9/85

AN HEIR FOR
THE WORLD'S
RICHEST MAN

AN HEIR FOR THE WORLD'S RICHEST MAN

MAYA BLAKE

MILLS & BOON

First published in Great Britain 2019
by Mills & Boon, an imprint of HarperCollins*Publishers*
1 London Bridge Street, London, SE1 9GF

Large Print edition 2019

© 2019 Maya Blake

ISBN: 978-0-263-08308-8

MIX
Paper from
responsible sources
FSC **FSC™ C007454**

This book is produced from independently certified
FSC™ paper to ensure responsible forest management. For
more information visit www.harpercollins.co.uk/green.

Printed and bound in Great Britain
by CPI Group (UK) Ltd, Croydon, CR0 4YY

To Dad.

For passing your love of books to me.

For setting me on my path to my true self.

For making me what I am today. An author.

I miss you. I thank you. Always and for ever.

CHAPTER ONE

SAFFRON EVERHART STARED at the obscenely large, hideously expensive bouquet of flowers on her desk and her heart dropped into her stomach. This was going to be much more difficult than she'd ever imagined.

Over the years she'd learned to decode the levels of hell associated with the gifts that arrived on her desk on any given day.

Flowers meant prepare not to sleep for the next seventy-two hours. Flowers and a gift certificate to the most exclusive spa in Switzerland meant pack a bag and have someone water your plants because you won't be going home for a week. The last circle of hell was reserved for flowers and *jewellery*. These days the sight of precious gems made her shudder. She had three diamond bracelets, a Harry Winston pink diamond necklace with matching earrings, and a diamond and sapphire brooch she absolutely hated the sight of simply because of the blood, sweat and tears they'd wrung from her.

So, in a way, the flowers, as breathtaking and stomach-hollowing as they were, were a blessing simply because they had no accompaniment.

Still…

She set the Waterford crystal vase down at the farthest corner of her desk, curbing the urge to caress the soft petals of the hothouse lilies she knew had come from a florist who catered to a handful of exclusive A-list clientele. Just as she resisted the urge to lean forward and inhale their bewitching midnight-breeze scent, or be bowled over by the knowledge that each of the thirty long stems in the gigantic vase cost over a thousand pounds.

She rose from her desk, ignoring the sensational view of London spread out in rare sun-splashed splendour below her, and pivoted to face the double doors of the office adjoining hers.

The breath she took was shaky and weak, her clammy hands and churning gut a world removed from the image she strove to achieve. The image her straight spine and impeccable clothes projected.

More and more, that set of doors had seemed like the summit of Everest, fraught with dangers that screamed at her to turn back. Except she couldn't.

Not just yet.

But she'd delayed enough. Two whole months to be exact. It was time to take the final step.

Time to put that one night, that astoundingly risky dive into temptation that had set in motion events that made her heart dip each time she allowed herself to think of it, behind her.

Time to take back control of her life before it was too late.

Before she could compel her feet to move, a knock on the outer door stopped her. She turned, her stomach dropping to her toes at the sight of the smartly dressed courier heading purposefully towards her. Bicycle couriers and messengers weren't allowed above the fifteenth floor. She was on the forty-ninth, one step from the highest floor in the building owned by the richest man in the world.

And the man who was heading her way reverently clutching a black velvet briefcase with the logo of the Queen's jeweller proudly emblazoned on it was the furthest you could get from an ordinary courier.

'No.' The word was ripped from her throat, accompanied by several self-preserving steps backward, because, unlike the tennis bracelets and the other priceless gifts, this jeweller, this *delivery* signalled a whole new playing field. The kind that warned you to kiss your soul goodbye.

That clammy hands and an inability to breathe properly would be the least of her worries if she gave into what was unfolding.

'No, no, *no*.'

The courier paused halfway to her desk, his gaze befuddled. 'Beg your pardon, miss? Do I have the wrong floor? I have a delivery for a Miss Everhart. Can you redirect me if this isn't the right office? I'm afraid I'll need a signature from her.'

She shook her head. 'No. I mean, yes, you're in the right office but, no, you don't need a signature. You won't need one because you won't be making a delivery.' She was aware her voice bordered on hysterical but she couldn't help it. 'The gift is being returned,' she added for complete and undeniable emphasis.

His nervousness increased. 'I'm afraid that won't be possible. There's a non-returnable, non-refundable condition attached to the gift.'

'That's not true,' she stated firmly. 'I'm Miss Everhart, and I've dealt with your establishment before. I know for a fact that's not the case.'

Sweat beaded on his forehead. Saffron almost felt sorry for him. 'Well…yes, miss, in most cases it is. But not this time.'

'Why not?' she demanded, but deep down, she knew the answer.

'Because the client specifically requested it.'

She resisted the urge to squeeze her eyes shut in panicked exasperation because...*of course he did*. The man could outthink the shrewdest opponent without breaking a sweat, could execute a dozen chess moves in a dozen games simultaneously while lounging behind his desk with his eyes shut. Why she'd think he wouldn't use such a contingency on this occasion was almost laughable.

But Saffron wasn't in the mood to laugh.

Her gaze dropped to the case, her stomach knotting tighter. If it'd held a nest of deadly scorpions, she would've been more welcoming.

The courier cleared his throat. 'If I may say so, Miss Everhart, this is no ordinary piece. I believe permission was sought, and given, by Her Majesty for her necklace to be replicated. It's one of the most exquisite pieces our establishment has had the privilege of creating.' His tone bordered on reverence, his bewilderment at her reaction evident.

She didn't doubt him. But the reason for its appearance in her life was blaring thunderously in her ears, blocking everything save for the fact that if she didn't refuse this, if she delayed taking control of her life, she would be lost for ever. She'd already given four years of her life. Lived on the edge of her emotions. She couldn't give another day. *Another minute.*

The man in front of her wasn't the problem, though. The man seated on his throne-like chair behind the grey steel doors twenty feet from her was.

With brisk efficiency that disguised the churning mix of panic and dread inside her, she signed the delivery document and took possession of the package, knowing in her heart that she was making a huge mistake.

The door shut behind the courier. Saffron remained rooted in place, the box growing heavier with each second. When she could bear it no longer, she returned to her desk, sat down heavily and opened it.

The tiered diamond and ruby necklace was flawless.

Breathtakingly beautiful in a way no blatant bribe from a ruthless, coldly dismissive man had the right to be. At least it wasn't a choker. That symbolism would've been a step too far.

She suppressed a hysterical laugh and stared, awed despite herself, at the most stunning piece of jewellery she'd ever seen in her life. Her fingers itched to caress the precious stones, to experience their sparkling beauty through touch as well as sight.

She snapped the box shut before temptation took hold, and, just like the flowers, set it out of arm's reach.

She couldn't...*wouldn't* be swayed.

For far too long she'd given herself a pass, let the irresistible enticements of her position, specifically her proximity to the most charismatic man she'd ever encountered, lead her towards that one final act of insanity.

Well...never again.

Jaw gritted in a futile effort to stop the electricity that zapped through her every time she recalled that fateful night in Morocco, she read through the document she'd redrafted a dozen times and hit print.

The whirring sound of the printer spitting out the single sheet was both reassuring and terrifying. She was finally doing this, taking the ultimate step. Soon, she would be in complete control of her life. But first, there was the small problem of getting over this last monumental hurdle.

Saffron had no doubt that it would be a formidable battle.

She picked up the paper, folded it in two and rose.

With a cursory knock, she entered the lion's

den. Just in time to hear the exclusive phone reserved for super-VIP clients ring.

She froze in the doorway, her breathing nosediving as her gaze landed on the man reaching for the silver phone.

Joao Oliviera.

Her boss.

The richest man in the world with looks far outmatching that awe-inspiring title.

Despite the innumerable times she'd entered his domain, Saffron had never quite mastered the awe that possessed her in his presence. She'd just learned to disguise it to the point where she could appear almost dismissive of the endless layers of the powerful, magnetic aura he exuded, the breath-stealing vitality of his six-foot-four frame, his innate ability to strike the most influential leaders dumb with a few well-placed words.

And the feverish electricity of his touch.

No amount of training or self-denial could disguise the fact that Joao Oliviera, with his obscene wealth and good looks, was Midas, Croesus and Ares rolled into one sublime package.

Thick dark brown hair, longer than conventionally acceptable and tipped with the faintest gold, gleamed in the May sunlight slanting through the glass window behind him.

Chiselled cheekbones drew immediate, captivating attention to the olive vibrancy of his face, the uncompromising line of an upper lip neatly counterbalanced by the sinful, sensual curve of his lower lip, and the rugged outline of his faintly shadowed jaw that no amount of shaving could completely smooth.

Startling whisky-gold eyes framed by long, spiked eyelashes completed the magnificent picture.

Those eyes flicked up at her entrance, studied her for a piercing second before he beckoned her with long, elegant fingers. As was his habit, he'd shed his jacket shortly after his day began, leaving the pristine white shirt and Italian-made silk vest that emphasised his racehorse-lean physique on full display.

It was early, barely eight o'clock on a Monday morning, so he hadn't got around to undoing his cuffs and folding back his shirtsleeves to reveal his brawny forearms. In the giant scheme of breathless hellishness, she took that as a blessing in disguise.

'Lavinia, I've been waiting for your call,' he drawled into the phone.

And just like that, Saffron was lashed by another whip of her most sinful craving. Over the years she'd battled to suppress her base reactions to almost everything about Joao—save for that one searing night in Morocco. His impressive mental dexterity, his jaw-dropping physique, his superhuman energy, the breathtaking ruthlessness wrapped around a core of unwavering integrity. But the one thing she'd never conquered was her reaction to the deep, intensely sexy, accented voice.

It shot arrows of flaming lust into her during her waking hours, and, with alarming frequency lately, invaded her dreams just as shamelessly. It'd reached the point where she almost dreaded walking into his office.

With any luck, she wouldn't have to suffer it for much longer.

Saffron shut the door behind her and tuned into the conversation. Regardless of her primary reason for coming into Joao's office, she had work to do. This morning—and, she suspected, countless more to come—that work involved Lavinia Archer.

At seventy-four, the head of the renowned Archer Group, an empire that comprised Archer Hotels, Archer Brewery, Archer Cruise Liners, Archer Airlines and several more offshoots, had been in control for over three decades.

When rumours had surfaced that Lavinia intended to sell her company to one buyer before her seventy-fifth birthday, Saffron had known it would be catnip to her boss. She'd been proved right when Joao had immediately set out to add the entire Archer empire, valued at thirty-one billion dollars, into his already staggering portfolio.

For the last three months, he'd woven an intricate web around Lavinia Archer, one involving a game of mental chess and charm that the older woman, despite courting several buyers, hadn't been able to resist participating in.

'I know you take pleasure in making me wait, Lavinia,' Joao continued, the timbre of his voice smooth, dark and potent like the special blend of coffee his handpicked aficionados cultivated for him exclusively in his native Brazil. Every word oozed effortless charisma as his dark golden gaze tracked Saffron across his office. 'I hope when the time comes, you'll let me make the climax worth your while.'

Saffron stumbled, briskly caught herself on the edge of the sectional sofa that graced the office, and dragged her gaze from his coolly mocking one before she compounded her rare clumsiness by blushing.

Sultry laughter flowed from the phone. Saffron curbed the irrational jealousy that welled inside her and attempted to maintain her composure.

Even though she'd given him four years of her life, when it came right down to it, she had no rights where Joao was concerned. He didn't care about her beyond her excellent organisational skills.

Not once had he asked her what her interests were outside the office—not that she had much time to pursue any of them. Her last two birthdays had passed her by because she'd been so engrossed in making Joao Oliviera's life problem-free that she'd missed them.

And the fact that there'd been no one else to remind her—no family, friends, nor even acquaintances—and that her boss hadn't known to treat those days differently from any other work-hard-and-then-even-harder days, had been just one of the many things that had bruised her deep inside when she'd finally girded her loins and taken stock of her life.

Unsurprisingly, all the things wrong with her life had been down to one man.

Joao Oliviera.

So, no, she wasn't going to waste a moment's energy on being jealous. And when she was done with her task here, he could charm the birds from the trees for all she cared. She wouldn't be around to see it. Wouldn't experience that stressful little pull in her chest when he arranged an assignation with the next supermodel or socialite.

Thankfully he hadn't done that since Morocco. Not to her knowledge anyway, which in no way proved conclusively that he hadn't—

Enough!

Interrupting her own spiralling thoughts, she refocused to find Joao's gaze raking over her body, lingering for a moment on the document in her hand before rising to meet her eyes.

Her heart lurched.

For the last eight weeks, he'd treated her with cool indifference. He'd watched her when he'd wanted to and ignored her when it had pleased him.

Saffie was forced to admit it was that detachment that had finally triggered her actions. That knowledge that she couldn't endure much more of this, couldn't pretend that her life hadn't boiled down to being an insignificant satellite that orbited around his brilliance.

That Morocco hadn't happened.

She pressed her lips together, fighting the chaotic sensations in mind and body as Joao let out a low, deep laugh.

'*Sim*, I'll respect you in the morning. You'll leave satisfied that your legacy is in the best hands possible.'

Long fingers tapped the smooth surface of his glass desk, drawing her attention to its graceful elegance, its subdued power. From there it was a mere skip to unlocking memories of when those fingers made firm, deliberate contact with her skin. Stroked and teased and branded, leaving an indelible mark on her.

She watched his arm rise, his fingers stretching out in silent command for the document.

While Joao's ability to multitask was another skilful feather in his cap, she hadn't anticipated executing this task while he conducted one of the biggest deals of his company's history.

But...the order of things didn't matter. She was here to take her life back.

So, do it.

Lips pressed firmly together, she handed over the paper.

Perhaps her expression gave her away. Perhaps the poker face that had seen her through four long years but had begun to crack after Morocco had finally let her down.

Seconds breathlessly ticked by as he continued to recite facts and figures to Lavinia in his deep accented voice, all without taking his eyes off Saffron's face. A full minute later, his gaze finally dropped to the sheet.

Shrewd eyes skimmed the document with

lightning speed. Then his breathtaking face tightened.

Her insides jumped as those hypnotic eyes rose to lock on hers.

'*Sim,*' he murmured smoothly to Lavinia, although Saffie heard curt edginess wrapped around the word. 'But remember I'm not a patient man. I want your company, and I will play your games for now. But eventually one of us will grow bored and resort to…other measures. Prepare yourself for that scenario, too, *meu querido*. Until the next time.'

The words might have been directed into the phone but Saffie felt their impact deep inside.

With a casual flick of his hand, he ended the call. Then chilled, narrowed eyes rose from her carefully crafted resignation letter to her face.

'What is the meaning of this?' he breathed in a low, deadly voice.

Saffron called on every last crumb of composure and held his stare. 'It's exactly as it says. I'm tendering my resignation.'

His gaze flickered with a hint of disbelief, then dropped to the page. 'For *"personal reasons"*? You do not have a personal life, therefore you cannot have personal reasons. *Therefore*—' he flicked a disdainful finger at the sheet '—this is a blatant lie.'

She didn't want to be hurt by the caustic words. By now, she should be immune to his brand of ruthless disregard for any impediment that stood between him and whatever goal he pursued. And yet that mysterious pang that had sprung up the morning after their fateful night burrowed deeper into her heart.

'Thank you so much for pointing that out. And while I'm at it, thank you for the flowers and jewellery, although I won't be accepting them. I'm assuming you're about to step things up with Lavinia, hence the need for that outrageous bribe?'

Not by a flicker of an eyelash did he acknowledge any wrongdoing in commissioning a necklace most monarchs would give an eye tooth for. 'You're building up to a point, I expect? Some sort of negotiation perhaps?' he mused.

'You're not going to give me the courtesy of an answer?'

'I believe one of the first things we discussed at the start of your employment was not to ask questions you already know the answers to. Would you like me to repeat mine? Because you haven't given me a satisfactory answer.'

'Every answer you need is in that letter. I'm resigning for personal reasons. Effective immediately after the requisite notice period.'

The gaze he flicked at the letter was filled with

such singeing disdain, Saffron was surprised it didn't catch fire.

'You're not flighty. You're supremely efficient. Dependable. Level-headed. One of the most hardworking people I know. In the past four years, there hasn't been a single task you haven't executed to my satisfaction,' he drawled, angling his body back to lounge in the high-backed, throne-like chair a vaunted French furniture designer had fashioned exclusively for him. The stance threw his gladiator-like frame into high-definition relief, the sunlight doing its part to showcase his perfect body.

Saffron's thighs snapped together as heat singed her feminine core and burrowed deep, sensuously, into her pelvis, reminding how it'd felt to have that body up close, personal...*naked*.

Inside her.

'Thank you. I'm glad you noticed.'

Her sarcasm went over his head. As with most things he thought beneath his regard. Why was she even surprised?

'Which is why I'm puzzled by your need to couch your so-called resignation in such...whimsical, flowery prose. You're *"honoured by the opportunity"* to have worked with me? You wish me *"the brightest of futures"*? Your experience with me will remain *"an unforgettable experience"*?' he recited.

Fine, so she'd let her nerves run away with her in the early hours of the morning when she'd redrafted the letter *yet again*, but did he really need to repeat it in such mocking tones? 'Believe it or not, everything on there is true—'

'Everything on here is nonsense!' His deep voice was a merciless scythe through her response. 'Your resignation is not accepted. Especially not at such a crucial point in my dealings with Lavinia. We've been going about this all wrong. It's time to flip the script. To win her over we have to show her what she *doesn't* know she's missing. Let's take her out of her comfort zone, in the most enticing way. You think you can handle that?'

Saffron fought the urge to clench her fists and stamp her foot. That would achieve absolutely nothing. Besides, as Joao had so coldly categorised, she wasn't flighty. She was dependable. Level-headed. Hard-working. *Obedient.*

Qualities she'd striven for as an orphan. Everything the nuns at St Agnes's Home For Children had assured her would secure foster parents and eventually parents who would adopt her, only for her to be passed over time and again in favour of others. She'd shed silent tears—because it wouldn't have done for Sister Zeta to hear her crying and be disappointed in her—when bratty Selena had been chosen instead of her that week before Christmas when she was seven.

She'd been overwhelmed with sorrow when eight months later another smiling couple had walked away with a child that wasn't her.

Through every heart-rending repetition of those events, she hadn't shown any outward sign of distress or, even worse, thrown a tantrum like some of the other children. Eventually when her moment had finally arrived at the ripe old age of fourteen, she had refrained from exhibiting any outward signs of elation, lest it be misconstrued.

She'd maintained that self-possession through the two happy years she'd spent with her foster mother, and then through the harrowing eighteen months when her health had rapidly declined. Saffie had kept tearless vigils by her bedside, made the solemn promise that, no, she wouldn't succumb to loneliness, that, yes, she would seek another family for herself when the time came, no matter what.

When, a week before her eighteenth birthday, Saffron had buried her foster mother, she'd buoyed up everyone at the small funeral gathering, recounting her fondest memories of that wonderful woman and drawing smiles to every-

one's faces. And she'd made sure she was completely alone before shedding a single tear.

It was near enough with that same composure
that she pivoted away from Joao's desk and returned to her desk. Where she placed a call to a
number she knew by heart.

Once the call was done, she reached for the
velvet box with not quite steady hands and returned to her boss's office.

'Are you coming down with an ailment?' Joao
demanded, a healthy dose of that Brazilian temper melting away a layer of indifference. 'Would
you like me to summon the company doctor for
you?'

'That won't be necessary. I'm absolutely fine.
In fact, I'm more than fine. I'm seeing things
a little more clearly for the first time in a long
while.'

He tensed, his eyes probing deeper. 'And those
things include resigning from a job that you
stated in your last evaluation was *"the most ful-
filling thing"* in your life?'

She bit the inside of her cheek, regret for those
exposing words drenching her. But again, it was
one of the many faults in her life she intended to
rectify sharpish. 'Yes.'

Tense seconds ticked by as he eyed her. 'You
do realise you could've stated a number of rea-

sons for resigning besides this *personal* excuse
you're holding so preciously to your chest?'

The observation stopped her short.

Had it been deliberate? Did she, on some sub-
liminal level, wish him to see beneath her façade, to the heart of her single, deepest desire?
To that yearning that had started with a death-
bed promise and blossomed soon after her foster mother's passing, when Saffron had realised
she was once again alone in the world, and had
known she wouldn't feel whole again until she
fulfilled it? A yearning that had momentarily
faded against the brilliant supernova that was
Joao, only to re-emerge invigorated, viscerally
demanding fulfilment?

No.

One night had been enough. The last thing
she wanted was to reveal any more of her vulnerabilities to a man like Joao Oliviera. A man
who breathed and bled commerce. A man who
dropped his lovers swiftly and without mercy
the moment they harboured the barest notions
of permanence. A man without a family and a
blatantly stated anathema towards ever encum-
bering himself with one.

'I was hoping you'd respect my privacy and
leave it at that.'

'We have never deluded one another, Saffie. Let us not start now.'

Her breath caught at the accented way he pronounced her shortened name. *Saahfie.*

Each time it sent electric shivers down her spine, made her breasts tingle and her belly flip-flop in giddy excitement. This time was no different despite the volatile tension arcing between them.

But his statement made her breath catch for different, more terrible, reasons.

She had lived through months, perhaps even years of delusion.

Ultimately, *that* shameful realisation that she was chasing dreams, and wasting precious time doing so, was why she stood before him now.

'Your letter threw up red flags. I'm acknowledging those flags and demanding to know what's going on. Especially since we parted company only a few hours ago and you gave no inkling of pulling this stunt.'

'Firstly, it's not a stunt. Secondly, did it occur to you that I might not want to do this for ever? You might imagine you have immortal blood flowing through your veins and are therefore going to live for ever. Some of us are more cognisant of our mortality. So pardon me if I've realised that I don't want to work until two a.m.

on a Monday morning only to turn around and return to the office at seven-thirty to put in another eighteen hours.'

A dark frown descended over his brows and something like disappointment shot through his eyes. For whatever reason his anger didn't grate as much as his disappointment. 'That's the problem? You're complaining about your workload? You have my permission to hire yourself another assistant.'

She eased her grip on the box, breached the last few steps to his desk and set it down. 'I can't accept this. Even if I weren't leaving, it would still be too much. I've donated the flowers to the gala organisers for the charity dinner you're attending this evening. Prepare for Lady Monroe's effusiveness when she sees you tonight. She believes they'll easily fetch twenty thousand pounds if they're auctioned off—'

'*Pelo amor de*—enough with this lifeless performance. Tell me what you want and let's get it out of the way so we can get back to work! Give away the flowers if you wish but the necklace is yours.'

'Joao—'

'It cannot be money. I already pay you ten times more than your closest rival. I'd offer to triple that salary but I suspect you'd say—'

'It's not money.'

He gave a brisk nod. '*Bom*, we're getting somewhere. What is it, then?'

Her heart stuttered. She couldn't tell him. Not everything and certainly not what had triggered her decision to walk away. His indifference since their night in Morocco had said everything.

At best, that disappointment on his face would deepen. At worse, he'd mock her for letting emotions get the better of her.

But she wasn't a robot.

Her life was flashing past before her eyes and she'd already given him more years than she'd originally planned. And with every day she sacrificed her innermost needs on the altar of Joao's newest business obsession, she despaired a little more.

And perhaps even hated him a fraction, too. For that indifference she knew would never change. For his inability to step down from his god-like throne and deign to acknowledge the needs of mere humans.

Her needs.

'You want to know why I'm leaving? It's simple. I've decided you're not the answer to my every problem.'

His eyes narrowed into dark gold slits. 'What

is that supposed to mean?' he snapped. 'Stop playing games and speak plainly!'

Irritation bristled through her. 'Or else what? You're going to stop me from walking out?'

Silence throbbed between them.

Slowly he rose, his impressive height dwarfing hers even from across the desk as he removed the cufflinks from his shirtsleeves, and meticulously folded them back.

She didn't want to watch, didn't want to acknowledge that extra dose of virile masculinity that made him impossible to ignore. But she couldn't help herself. Her gaze dropped to follow every inch of silky-hair-dusted forearms that was exposed. Tiny lightning bolts fired through her, blazing her already aggravated libido as she wondered how those strong arms would feel banded around her waist again, drawing her close to the towering perfection of his hard, muscled body.

'What is going on, Saffie?' The low-voiced demand, wrapped in power and authority, jerked her from her lustful reverie.

Her fingers gripped the straps of her handbag. At no point had she deluded herself that resigning as Joao's executive assistant after living and breathing the role for four full-on years would be easy. But she hadn't anticipated it being this *hard* either. If he'd shown zero interest in her life outside the walls of his existence before Morocco, he'd been a million times more detached since.

He didn't know about her childhood in the orphanage, about her short, happy spell with her foster mother. About her devastation when she'd been orphaned once again.

About the promise she'd made.

Her heart thundered as she panicked that he wouldn't let go until she gave him something. She didn't realise she was slicking a nervous tongue over her bottom lip until his gaze dropped to her mouth.

For a single moment, detachment vanished.

Then it returned full force, bruising her with its severity.

'Do you remember how I came to be your assistant in the first place?' Saffie asked, needing temporary relief from this quagmire.

His frown intensifying, he dropped the cufflinks in a drawer and slammed it shut. 'I fail to see how that's relevant.'

'It's relevant to me. I was supposed to be here temporarily, while my old boss, Mr Harcourt, was on holiday. You'd just fired your own assistant, remember?'

'Barely. I'm still not seeing how this is material—'

'My point is, I was supposed to be here for *two*

weeks. I've been here for four years. And by the way, is it true you offered Mr Harcourt early retirement so you could keep me here?'

Again, he didn't so much as blink. '*Sim.* I knew by the end of your first week that you were far more suited to me. Your talents were wasted creating company retreat spreadsheets so I made him an offer he couldn't refuse,' he said with zero remorse.

'Well… I'm glad that's out of the way.'

His jaw gritted but a wary gleam entered his eyes. A gleam that said he was realising that this wasn't a tantrum or a stunt. That she might actually mean it. 'Now that we've wandered uselessly down memory lane, can we get back on track? What would it take for you to end this? Name your price and I'll make it happen.'

Name your price.

If only she could.

If only she didn't know the futility of naming her *actual* price.

She stared at him, her heart hammering as it had every time she'd contemplated taking this final step.

Granted, the thought that she would one day soon wake up and not be in his presence left her bereft. But then she forced herself to think of what else she would be replacing that experience with. The fulfilment her heart and soul yearned for. A true connection. A life-affirming purpose. 'My price is my freedom, Joao. I gave you two weeks, then I added four years to that. Now I want out.'

Leisurely he leaned forward, his bronzed forearms rippling as he resettled his weight on his hands, brought that red-hot sensuality dangerously closer, and glared at her across the desk. 'You have one last chance to give me a clear, concise reason for this absurdity, Saffie.'

The urge to tussle with him sizzled bright and urgently within her. What did she have to lose? In a few short weeks, she'd be out of his life. He planned to conquer the world, while she planned to retreat from his orbit, hopefully to embark on a lifelong project her soul had screamed for since she was a child. Since she'd tasted loneliness and vowed to make her life more meaningful.

Once she was done with Joao, she highly doubted their paths would ever cross again.

Ignoring the twinge in her chest, she boldly stepped forward, placing both feet on the battle ground. 'Very well. You want the unvarnished truth? You're a brilliant businessman, Joao. But you're also a ruthless vampire. You take and you take, and you think throwing diamonds and flowers and unimaginable perks grants you automatic authority over my life. Well, it doesn't. I mapped out a path for myself when I joined your company. I put my plans on hold and now I'm making them a priority again. I'm resigning because I want more. More from *life*. I want freedom from being *consumed* by you. Freedom to dream of other things besides the acquisition of your next *Fortune 500* company. Freedom to dream of a family. A baby. Of turning that dream into a reality.' She paused, her insides shaking at the thought of taking that last, intensely ravaging but *necessary* step. 'I want freedom from *you*.'

CHAPTER TWO

SILENCE PULSED IN the aftermath of his executive assistant's terse monologue. Joao, stunned into uncharacteristic silence, coldly ticked off the myriad sensations zipping through him.

Shock. Banked fury.

Hardened disappointment.

Perplexity.

It was to that last one that he returned. That feeling of being caught off guard when he'd believed them to be perfectly in sync.

He stared at her, wondering whether this was her idea of a joke. But then his level-headed, capable assistant didn't joke. They didn't have that kind of relationship. Theirs was a well-oiled symbiosis that ran on a perfect synergy of efficiency, a mutual appreciation of hard work and the heady rewards and satisfaction of success.

At least it had.

Until that night when, drunk on success, their basest instincts had got the better of them. But they'd put that behind them. Saffie's work hadn't suffered. On the contrary, things had been better than ever. Granted, the first week after the Morocco incident he'd lived on tenterhooks, wondering if she would attempt to capitalise in some way on his error of judgement. Because giving in to uncontrolled hunger *had* been an error of judgement. Other men might approach lust with a cavalier attitude, but Joao Oliviera was singularly ruthless when it came to his bed partners. They were chosen strictly on a mutually agreed short-term basis from which he never strayed.

They weren't chosen based on an unexpected but breathtaking desert mirage come to life, a punch of unstoppable lust that had nearly felled him and deep, dark craving that had blinded him to common sense until it was too late.

The fact that it'd happened, that for the space of one night he'd been no better than the man he despised the most in his life, still had the power to sour his day.

Sure, he hadn't gone looking for it, and Saffron wasn't a hooker on a street corner, but the acute absence of control still left a bitter aftertaste in his mouth.

Fortunately, like him, she'd been only too happy to bury the incident in the past. And while the realisation had initially grated, he'd eventually welcomed that discretion.

So what if the experience had the unsavoury ability to replay in his memory when he least expected it? What if those memories left him aroused and aching at the most inappropriate times?

It had rightly stayed in the past where it belonged, never to be repeated.

Except for some reason, while he'd believed his world was back on an even keel, Saffie had been making other plans.

Plans that threatened to wreak havoc on the most crucial undertaking of his life.

Suppressing his fury, he searched her face. Read the fierce determination on it and realised she actually meant it.

She meant to leave him. To free herself so she could chase so-called dreams.

For a family.

A baby.

She inhaled sharply and he realised he'd spoken the words out loud. Spat out, like one of the few foreign languages he wasn't fluent in. Two terse words tossed out like the vile, bewildered curse he believed them to be because they had no place in his working day.

In his life.

Not since the day he'd wiped the word *family* from his soul.

Certainly not now when his goal was so close. When the chance to shatter his enemy once and for all was a mere handful of weeks away.

That off-kilter sensation deepened, that feeling of being flung unexpectedly into a turbulent ocean without a life jacket causing his gut to clench.

He had countless life jackets. Endless contingencies to ensure not a single thing in his life was irreplaceable. Yachts and planes and CEOs and leaders of the free world, all at his beck and call.

Except Saffron Everhart had carved out a unique place in his life, set herself up on a pedestal marked exactly that. *Irreplaceable.*

And now that he needed her most...

He whirled away from his desk, strode to the wide floor-to-ceiling windows where he usually took one of his many espressos as he juggled the demands of his empire. He breathed through the tension riding his frame, his brain already in counter-strategy mode.

'Let me get this straight. You're ditching your career, and the countless benefits that come with it, to what? Go on some journey of self-discovery?' he threw at her.

She took her time to answer. Time that grated

along his nerves, fired up his already smouldering discontent.

It didn't help that he usually welcomed her thoughtful consideration when answering his questions. That she wasn't the type to blurt out the first thought in her head as some people did.

'Yes, Joao. If you want to drill it down to one oversimplified statement. I'm leaving for me but I'm not ditching my career. Far from it. You can pour scorn all you want on it but my mind is made up. I have eight weeks of accrued vacation. I can stay and help train your next assistant or—'

He whirled to face her, a savage urgency *to do something* ripping through him. 'You're getting ahead of yourself. I haven't agreed that you can leave,' he bit out.

Her chin lifted. 'Then it's a good thing there are laws in this country preventing you from holding me in a job I don't want any more, isn't it?'

He smiled a smile he didn't feel. 'You wish to take me on in court?'

'If you drive me to it, absolutely.'

Again, the absolute certainty that she meant it ploughed a jagged path through him. Something about the way she was holding herself, boldly meeting his gaze where others would've backed down, fired up a much different sensation in him.

It…drew him.

Otherwise why did he find himself standing in front of her, his gaze tracing the delicate lines of her throat, when he was across the room moments ago?

He smashed the sensation down and drilled deeper into the subject at hand.

'When I said you were getting ahead of yourself, Saffie, I meant that we hadn't exhaustively discussed the subject you just dropped in my lap. What do you mean, you're not ditching your career? You're going to work for someone else?'

She blinked. Attempted to regroup. 'Well… yes, I am.'

'Who?' he fired back.

'It doesn't matter—'

'Of course, it matters. Who is it, Saffie?' At her hesitation, the churning in his gut intensified. 'Tell me now,' he breathed.

Her stubborn chin tilted higher, daring him in ways Joao wasn't sure he wanted to discover. 'It's William Ashby.'

As competitors went, this one wasn't a worthy one. Which absurdly infuriated him further. That she would leave him for someone significantly inferior businesswise… 'I didn't think you foolish, Saffie.'

'Excuse me?'

'Do you really think I'll allow you to take a position with my competitor, knowing what you know about my company?'

Twin flickers of anger and hurt darted across her face. 'You think I'll break your confidence? After…' She stopped herself but he already knew.

Wasn't this a subject *he'd* dwelt on for far too long in the past few weeks?

'After what?' he taunted. 'After *Morocco*? Or are we finally getting to the heart of this little scene?'

She blinked, shook her head, drawing his attention to the rich gloss of her hair. What it'd felt like tumbling freely over him—

'No, we're not. I don't want to talk about it.'

'Well, I do. Tell me Morocco is not why you've dropped this bombshell on my day and we can move on. And no, we won't be moving onto this so-called dream of a family or child because we both know you don't even have a boyfriend.'

Fire sparked in her eyes. 'What makes you think you know everything about me?'

Her spirited reply drew him even closer. He

rounded his desk, closed the gap between them, felt tendrils of her light floral perfume wrapping around him. 'You've been in charge of organising my life for over four years. That means I'm equally aware of yours and it isn't that much of a secret, Saffie—'

'I beg to differ or you would've seen this coming, wouldn't you?'

Joao took a breath. This wasn't working. For whatever reason, his assistant seemed hell-bent on this path. This unsatisfactory desire to leave him high and dry at this most crucial juncture of his life.

'You wish me to apologise for what happened in Morocco?'

Her eyes widened, the deep pools of blue pulling him in. 'What? No. I said—'

'I'm aware of what you said. Just as I'm aware what women tend to say often differs from what they truly mean.'

Her eyes flashed. 'Sorry to disabuse you of the notion but I'm not like your other women. I'm not hiding behind some nefarious ulterior motive. And while it may bruise your ego to hear the word no for the first time in your life—'

'Watch it, Saffie.'

She carried on regardless. 'That's exactly what

I'm saying. I don't want to be your assistant any more. My life is my own. I can do whatever I want. You have my letter. I've been in touch with HR. As soon as you accept, they'll get my termination papers ready.'

She turned on her heel, presenting him with the rigid curve of her spine that again commanded his attention to the curve of her hips, the tempting swell of her bottom.

He cursed under his breath. 'Aren't you forgetting something?' The arctic snap in his voice froze her in place.

Giving him the time he needed to stride over to join her at the door.

They weren't done. Far from it. He needed her far too much to let her walk out of his office.

Perhaps it was their close proximity that made her pulse race in her throat as she stared at him. Perhaps it was because she sensed he was about to pull out the big guns, as he was wont to do when the occasion demanded it.

Whatever the reason, he watched her drag her inner lip between her teeth, felt the unwelcome sensation deep in his pelvis.

Meu Deus. He needed to put this thing to bed, pronto.

'What?' she blurted.

'There's a clause in your contract that states all future employers will be vetted and approved by me. Tell me, do you think I'll let you run off and work for Ashby?'

The demand was soft. So soft Saffie didn't feel the warm knife slide into her ribs until it was too late.

'Why are you doing this?'

'Because I wish to keep the best personal assistant I've ever had.'

There was a time when the flippant compliment would've lit up her day. Not any more. 'I'm sure the next will do just as well.'

His nostrils flared. 'You can have an extended vacation after we put the Archer deal to bed.'

'Joao—'

'I will get my pilot to fly you to any destination of your choosing. You have my word that I won't ask you to return until you're well rested and you've worked whatever…lingering discontentment you have out of your system. Whatever it takes to get my level-headed executive assistant back.'

Despite his more than generous offer, the words dropped like icy bullets from his lips, his body language broadcasting his extreme displeasure.

The intimacy of his proximity and the sheer headiness of his masculine scent sent heat blooming through her as he continued to stare her down, reminding her that she hadn't always been level-headed.

She'd slipped and fallen from grace in Morocco.

His gaze dropped to her mouth, stayed and for a second she knew he was recalling it, too.

Then she realised she was full-on gnawing at her lip.

Her renowned rock-solid composure was slipping and, for the life of her, she couldn't get herself under control.

'I told you. I can't stay here and get what I want.'

His eyes narrowed. 'This accusation interests me greatly. Tell me on what basis you arrived at it,' he invited silkily.

'I've worked with you for four years. You might be progressive with your other employees, but I know, for instance, that the subject of families and babies doesn't interest you.'

One eyebrow spiked. 'You know this for a fact when you and I have never discussed it?'

'We may not have, but I've been present when business acquaintances have brought up the subject. Your eyes glaze over and you change the topic as soon as possible.'

One thick shoulder rose and fell. 'Because the subject of other people's children bores me,' he stated coldly.

Saffie forced herself to breathe through the sharp pang of hurt. 'Well, if you'll be so kind as to step out of my way, I'll stop boring you.'

She went to move around him. His hand whipped out and captured her wrist. Heat blazed from the contact, raining sharp tingles and making her gasp, this time for a completely different reason.

At the very top of her list—and underscored in indelible ink—of ways to avoid her tightly reined composure slipping around Joao was to never come into direct physical contact with him.

She'd learned that lesson in one sizzling, unforgettable way.

The Montcrief Pipeline deal.

The months' long negotiations for the Brazilian-Canadian deal had left her with little sleep and living on the very edge of her nerves alongside Joao.

Her usually unflappable boss had been like a man possessed, his focus on securing the multi-billion-dollar contract razor-sharp.

It was the first time the name Pueblo Oliviera

had truly registered. The first time she'd witnessed something other than the fervent need to bag the best deal. It'd been clear Montcrief was personal for Joao.

It hadn't taken a genius to connect the dots and conclude that he wanted to win against Pueblo Oliviera.

His father.

Joao had not only bagged the Montcrief deal, he'd signed another multibillion-dollar deal that had granted him ownership of his third premier soccer team in Brazil.

The double-barrelled success against his father had triggered a euphoric celebration, Joao's breathtaking exclusive Marrakesh villa and its grounds the scene of one of the most sophisticated parties Saffie and the entire executive staff had ever attended.

It had been there, surrounded by flame throwers, jugglers and exotic belly dancers, that she'd given in to illicit temptation, one that she couldn't recall without her stomach flipping and her skin burning with remembered excitement.

She wished she could blame it on one too many glasses of the Krug Clos d'Ambonnay, two thousand dollars per bottle, which had been flowing at the party.

Or the singular thrill of attempting her first belly dance, dressed in the midriff-baring costume and exotic jewellery that had made her feel feminine and sexy.

No.

It had been the expression on Joao's face when she'd looked up and found him leaning against a stone pillar, staring at her, the euphoric glaze of success glinting in his eyes.

It had been the unfettered excitement at seeing the heat in his eyes flame brighter as she'd swayed towards him.

And it had been the absolute rapture at the thickly muttered Portuguese words and searing brand of his touch when he'd jerked her close, stared down at her for a charged minute before kissing her with a sizzling intensity she'd never experienced before.

The kiss, the fever it'd sparked in her bloodstream, and the urge to taste danger, *just once*, had been too heady to deny. So when he'd swept her off her feet, she'd willingly twined her arms around his neck. When he'd walked away from the party, marched them up to his master suite and kicked the door shut, she'd almost wept with anticipation.

And when she'd finally known what it felt like

to be the lust-drunk focus of Joao's attention, what it felt like to be completely possessed by him, she'd feared her life would never be the same.

She'd been right.

'You are not other people. You don't bore me, Saffie. Quite the contrary.' His growled words slammed her to the present.

To the reminder that the morning after that night in Morocco, Joao had greeted her with stinging indifference. As if what had happened was of little consequence to him.

Then and now.

Her pulse hammered against the fingers curled around her flesh. And she died a little knowing he could feel it, too. 'What's that supposed to mean?'

His gaze shifted to where he held her, to where his thumb was moving slowly, seductively across her skin. 'You are my right hand,' he said, his accent thickening ever so slightly. 'One of the most important cogs in my business wheel. I would be a fool to let such an asset walk away. But if you need to hear the words, I value you for your intellect. Which is far from boring.'

Cog. Business. Asset.

Cold labels that spelled out all she would ever be to Joao. From the beginning she'd known that.

Somewhere along the line she'd finally accepted it. So why did the words douse her with such icy, isolating coldness?

Joao Oliviera was the biggest shark in an immense ocean. And as with all sharks there would come a day when she would become his prey. When he would chew her up and spit her out without so much as a blink of his whisky-gold eyes before moving on. She had enough sense to rescue herself before that happened. Especially when she had a goal much closer to her heart.

'You're really determined to do this? To walk out on your career?' he pressed.

She found the strength to reconnect with his gaze. 'To leave you, yes.'

He stared at her for a long, unblinking minute before eyes that were far too shrewd leisurely travelled over her body. They lingered at the frantic pulse beating at her throat, the agitated rise and fall of her chest she couldn't quite control, the dark purple silk of her blouse, right down to her legs and shoes before travelling back up again. This time they lingered on her hips, then her breasts, causing her flesh to tingle.

Reprieve came in the form of the phone on his desk ringing. Her inbuilt work ethic kicked in and she automatically glanced at it.

'Leave it,' he instructed gruffly. 'One of your assistants can get it.'

Very early on, she'd realised the sheer volume of work Joao produced meant she had to delegate less-sensitive work to others and she'd hired two assistants who answered to her.

He leaned closer, wrapped her tighter in his intoxicating scent. 'And nothing I can say can change your mind?' His tone had turned deadly silky, the kind that could weave spells around her.

She shook her head. Nowhere on their trajectory did their interests collide. It was why it'd taken her years to summon up the strength to walk away.

The breakneck lifestyle Joao led was no place to make long-term plans. Certainly not one that included her yearning for a family of her own. A baby.

How many times had she booked a ski trip to Aspen only for him to ski one black run and decide he would much prefer the slopes in Switzerland, preferably that same day?

Hadn't he woken her up in the middle of the night only a month ago and ordered her to arrange a tour of the Chilean vineyard he'd just purchased on the spur of the moment for forty million dollars? She had still been rubbing the sleep from her eyes when his private jet had taken off from his Greek island fifty minutes later.

And this relentless, *sizzling* awareness of him surely couldn't be good for her health?

No, she couldn't put this off any longer.

'No. There's nothing you can say to make me change my—'

'I know this is about Morocco. Specifically *the sex* we had in Marrakesh, is it not?' he enquired with a low, terse rumble that resonated deep inside her.

Saffie sagged against the door, very much aware her mouth was agape. 'What?' she murmured with a voice that didn't sound like her own.

'You can put it out of your mind, Saffie. It was a mistake that shouldn't have happened. If you need it to satisfy you so you stay, then have my apologies,' he continued tersely, his body held in military rigidness that didn't in any way detract from the mouth-watering package.

'I… No,' she strained out.

Latin temper flared in his eyes. 'You don't accept my apology? Or is it the veracity of it you doubt?'

She almost laughed.

Joao was a great many things—ruthless, acerbic to the point of cruel sometimes, impossibly arrogant. Too damn good-looking for words. But in all his dealings, he had never spoken a word he didn't mean. His core of integrity was the reason less powerful men envied him almost as much as they feared him. It was the reason she loved her job even when he slave-drove her to the brink of sanity sometimes. There was a synergy in their dynamic, a thrill that came from working so close to a brilliant mind that she never got bored with.

'No, it's not that,' she stated.

She couldn't stay.

This man was so dangerously intoxicating every atom in her body shrieked at her that anything other than walking away would be a mistake.

The Archer deal would be done in three months, sooner if Joao's single-minded determination bore fruit.

But at what ultimate cost to her?

Her breath shuddered out.

Too high. The penalty would be too high.

He nudged her chin up with one finger, compelling her to meet his eyes once more. The dual thrill of touch and stare dragged her deeper into the cauldron of temptation.

'Three months, Saffie. That is all I ask. Stay.

Finish the deal with me. Then leave if you insist,' he urged with a mesmerising drawl.

Three months. Not an eternity in the grand scheme of things, but, if she was having a hard time walking away now, how would it be in three months, knowing she'd once again put off pursuing the one thing that was so precious and close to her heart?

She couldn't.

She sucked in a breath, the action bringing her far too close to his solid heat and the earthy, evocative scent she knew didn't come from the grooming products his French *parfumier* specially designed for him and him alone. She knew it because one of her many, endless tasks was to pack for him and she'd given into a weak moment very early on and taken a long inhale of his aftershave. And then spent far too long after that attempting to decipher where that scent ended and his unique musk began.

She would probably never know.

Before the alarming weakness could totally take over her body, she turned blindly towards the door.

'Saffie.' Her name was a low growl. 'Where are you going?'

'Out for air. Or back to my desk. Either way my answer is still no.'

Her hand latched on the door but the heaviness of his silence stopped her from opening it. She fought a fierce battle against the need to turn, see his reaction to her response. But she was too scared. Silence meant that algorithm that passed for his brain was recalibrating, recalculating a way to get what he wanted.

Still, she wasn't prepared for the words that came next.

'I need you.'

Her lips parted in a stunned gasp. In four long years she'd never heard him utter those words. To her. To anyone. Joao wasn't a man who needed.

He wanted. He desired. He took.

She spun around, her stunned senses seeking an explanation on his enigmatic face. 'Are you manipulating me, Joao?'

Feet planted apart, hands on lean hips, his stare undaunted and unwavering, 'I want you to stay,' he stated with that brutal honesty that often disarmed and weakened an opponent before he went in for the kill. 'I'll do anything to achieve that. It also helps that you know me better than anyone else will in this lifetime.'

Swiftly she added that vital little extra needed to put the right spin on his words.

When it comes to business.

When it came to anticipating his needs and

ensuring he had every last detail of a deal at his fingertips, she was second to none.

She was even exceptional at reading between the lines of his latest private liaisons and, more often than not, guessing when it was time to put together the staggeringly expensive it's-been-fun-but-now-it's-over package that soothed the most desolate of broken hearts.

But until recently she'd painstakingly safe-guarded herself against the pitfalls of deeper emotional curiosity, had deliberately stopped herself from digging into the personal details that had seen Joao Oliviera dig himself out of a *favela* in Brazil to become one of the most powerful men in the world. Sure, the media had endless reports on his past and his page on the company website featured a three-paragraph bio, but besides a mother who'd reportedly died at a young age of thirty-five, there was very little else.

She had no idea what his favourite colour was, what had caused the deep, three-inch scar across his left palm, or where he went when he bade her a curt goodnight on Christmas Eve and disap-peared for twenty-four hours. The holiday was the only day in the year when her phone didn't ring with endless demands from him.

All she knew was that Joao was driven by a

rabid intensity that bordered on the obsessive. Self-preservation dictated that she take herself out of his orbit.

'I don't know you, Joao. Not really. And there's nothing wrong with wanting to take a different path to achieve my goals.'

A muscle rippled in his jaw. 'You thrive on the challenges I grant you, Saffie. You'll be bored rigid in the slow lane.'

She couldn't lie. In the past four years he'd shown her a lifestyle that most people tried to conjure in their wildest dreams and fell far short of. She'd seen the world many times over, had watched as he'd conquered it over and over again. Not to mention earning enough money and benefits to not need to work again for the rest of her life if she lived a quiet, uneventful existence.

She dismissed the dreary sensation that thought triggered, reminding herself that life would be far from dull with a baby in it.

'My mind is made up, Joao. I'll stretch out my four weeks' notice period to six if—'

The imperious slash of his hand chopped off her response. 'I don't want you here with one foot out the door. I need you here, fully committed to the Archer deal. To me.'

'What if this deal drags out longer than three months?'

'It won't. But be warned, Saffie. This is the last time I will ask.'

That final gauntlet snatched her breath from her lungs.

Saffie couldn't deny that the thought of waking up without the adrenaline buzz of plugging herself into Oliviera Enterprises and Joao's world had left her curiously empty, her horizon a grey landscape with only the glowing mirage of a baby to sustain her.

Granted, that glow had grown, the craving for a family she'd ignored for years suddenly rearing its head on her twenty-eighth birthday, reminding her that time was slipping through her fingers.

Her emotional well had been left depleted for the better part of half her life. She'd needed to put her emotions aside to nurse her foster mother through the long months of ill health and her eventual death. After that she'd shut herself off, unwilling to delve into her grief for fear she'd never find her way back out of the dark tunnel.

Ironically, it had been a terrifying incident on Joao's private jet and the emergency landing in Canada in the first year of her working for him that had forced her to confront her grief. Joao had given her a rare day off, believing it was the incident that had left her shaken and withdrawn.

She'd spent it mourning the foster parent who'd come into her life late and exited far too early. It'd also shone a very harsh, self-reflecting light on the emptiness in her life. One she hadn't wanted to face after that first, soul-destroying glimpse.

Luckily, having fallen in love with her new job, she'd been able to bury the emptiness. It hadn't stayed buried. And with each passing year, the light had burned brighter until she couldn't ignore the ache any more.

But while she'd experienced a soul-shaking satisfaction to be finally moving forward with her dream, hadn't a part of her also felt a little shame that the dream she'd held onto for so long no longer felt enough? That a different yearning burned just as bright and it was all her fault for nurturing it?

She stared at Joao, caught the ferocious swell of determination in his eyes. They could part on acrimonious terms with a possibility of an employment tribunal in her future—depending on how difficult he chose to be. Or she could have twelve unforgettable, stimulating weeks with the most charismatic man she was likely to encounter in her whole lifetime, while guarding the deeper yearning in her heart.

'I want to hear it, Saffie,' Joao pressed again,

spotting her weakening and going for the kill. 'Three months of your undivided attention on the Archer deal with no talk of leaving.'

She swallowed, attempted to think through the euphoric haze shrouding her common sense. 'Fine. I'll stay until the Archer deal is done.'

Joao didn't gloat.

What he did was stand to his full, imposing height, his gaze raking her frame, lingering on her hips, her breasts, before reconnecting with hers. Something shifted in his eyes, a calculating gleam that sent a spark of apprehension down her spine.

'And, Joao?'

'Sim?' he prompted, intent eyes fixed on her as a muscle ticced in his jaw. 'What is it?'

'I want your word that you won't stand in my way when the time comes.'

CHAPTER THREE

HE HAD WHAT he wanted.

She was staying. He'd bought himself the time to formulate a plan to rid himself of this issue of her leaving.

His agreement was all that was required.

And yet the *yes* that should've fallen from his lips stuck in Joao's throat, his satisfaction at heading off disaster laced with something he couldn't quite decipher.

Uncertainty, he finally decoded.

She had pulled the proverbial rug from beneath his feet and now he was uncertain where he stood.

Perhaps he was better off setting her free so she could go and play happy families with some faceless stranger…

The harsh rejection of that idea stopped him cold.

Absurd. The whole discussion from start to finish was absurd.

He shouldn't be aggravated this much by the

whole thing. Not when, as Saffie had pointed out, he had zero interest in most of the reasons she'd stated for her desire to leave.

While he didn't want a child or, heaven forbid, a *family*, since he'd permanently erased that idea out of his life's mission very shortly after his tenth birthday and not once spent a second reconsidering it, he'd accommodated others' desire for it, if barely. The right gift baskets and monetary bonus found their way to each employee on the announcement of a child's birth.

So why did the thought of his executive assistant taking a similar path grate so much? Why did the thought that one day in his future Saffie might exercise her right to walk away permanently trigger nothing but cold dread?

The answer blazed through him a second later.

Because he wasn't ready to let her go.

Her value had multiplied over the years. And what was he if not a man who capitalised on the value of his assets?

He'd simply been caught off guard. He'd spent far too long putting out this fire when he should've been behind his desk, formulating better plans to add the Archer Group to his portfolio.

Just as he'd spent far too many years moulding Saffron Everhart into the perfect right hand to release her prematurely from her role.

Right or wrong, and while he knew that, ultimately, he couldn't stop her, she belonged to him—

'Do you agree?'

Her husky voice cut through his thoughts, retraining his focus on her.

The heat that lanced his groin was shockingly brazen and had grown in intensity ever since *that night*. The one he'd spent long weeks afterwards fighting to forget without success.

He'd ruthlessly disguised that hunger, enough to even take pride in his ability to watch her walk into his office without showing that he was losing his mind to that immediate groin-stirring arousal. And yes, it'd infuriated him to know his success in wrestling down his carnal demon had been fed by Saffie's own easy dismissal of the incident.

'Joao?'

He gritted his teeth, wishing he hadn't insisted she address him by his first name shortly after she'd started working for him. Of course, he hadn't divulged the fact that he detested his surname but had hung onto it purely to show Pueblo Oliviera that he wouldn't be dismissed as easily as it'd taken him to instruct his security to throw him out of his Sao Paolo mansion that fateful day two decades ago. Never mind that he'd hated his mother for saddling him with the name of a man who'd had zero interest in assuming the role of fatherhood.

'Are we going to discuss this or are you going to keep staring at me like I've grown an extra set of eyes?' Saffie questioned briskly.

He shook off the sticky vines of his past and focused on her eyes. Alternately blue or grey depending on her clothing or mood, the wide, almond shapes were clear and direct. Intelligent. *Alluring.* As arresting as her full Cupid's-bow lips currently pressed into a prim line beneath her pert nose. They hadn't been so prim when he'd tasted them. They'd been soft, supple, mind-alteringly delicious when she'd parted them beneath his, gasped her pleasure, screamed her climax—

He flicked that torrid recollection away before it wreaked havoc on his groin. 'You seem so certain of the future, Saffie. What makes you think you won't be begging me to let you stay in three months' time?'

Her breath caught, alerting him to the fact that his tone had been harsher than he'd intended.

At his continued stare, she bit her lip just as

she had minutes ago, exhibiting an agitation unlike her.

Joao's attention was once again drawn to her perfect curve of slightly reddening mouth, to the small teeth dragging over her flesh. He clenched one fist over the other as more blood rushed south.

'I know what I want,' she insisted, once again triggering that unnerving sensation that had arrived when he'd read that damn resignation letter and felt the searing vacuum of her loss.

His teeth gritted but he saw no way to deny her. '*Bom.* Then you have my word. Now can we get back on track?'

Despite the telltale sign of her less than cool state, her eyes boldly met his as she nodded and quickly regrouped. It made him wonder how often his seemingly unflappable assistant had stumbled and corrected course without him noticing.

'I'll draw up the list you requested.'

'Good. Did you like the necklace I commissioned for you?' he asked as she opened her door.

Wary blue eyes met his. 'Yes, it's stunning—'

'Now that you're staying, I'd very much like for you to wear it when we attend the auction of the Shanzi orchid in Shanghai with Lavinia

Archer. Unless you're going to argue with me over that, too?'

She exhaled calmly, not rising to his bait. He should've been glad his EA was back to her unflappable self. But he wasn't. Not completely.

'We've reached an agreement, Joao. Things will run as normal for the duration. I'll ensure your plate is clear and Lavinia is free to be in Shanghai so you can present her with the orchid, which will bloom, for the first time in eight years, two weeks from now. Was there anything else?'

Her question contained more than a spark left over from their encounter and Joao was almost tempted to stoke it.

But enough.

Now he'd put out this little fire of her intended desertion he needed to refocus on his father. Specifically ensuring Pueblo didn't come out the victor in their battle to win Lavinia Archer's business.

Dark anticipation twisted with bitterness in Joao's gut. These days the man who'd fathered him might still call himself a billionaire but Joao's was the Oliviera name people uttered in deference and awe. It was he world leaders turned to for business and geo-political counsel.

Joao knew it stuck in Pueblo's craw that the

bastard son he'd cursed to damnation, the product of a drunken indulgence with a prostitute one wholly forgettable night, had become a man of untold power and means. It was a status his father was desperate to overturn.

In turn, Joao intended to devote his time and effort to maintaining his superior position. To do that he needed his sharpest players, including his right hand, in their rightful place.

So he reined himself in but not before he went to his desk, picked up her resignation letter and ripped it in two.

'You may take this with you.' He held it out to her, watched her retrace her steps to where he stood next to his desk.

The sway of her hips reminded him that he hadn't indulged himself for several weeks. Not since Morocco. Not since that night he'd celebrated his victory over his father with a tumble into temptation and awoken to learn of Pueblo's interest in the Archer Group.

And he wouldn't indulge himself for a while yet. Not if he didn't want to lose his way and lose this fight. He knew first-hand what chaos unbridled lust could create.

He had no intention of falling into that trap again.

With enviable composure, Saffie took the

ripped page from him. 'If that's all, I'd like to go and get on with the day?'

'By all means,' he murmured.

He watched her walk briskly out of his office, feeling as if he'd freshly emerged from an industrial-sized centrifuge.

Sure, some of the spur-of-the-moment deals he'd capitalised on had been the best of his life... but had any of them left him reeling like this?

And all over his assistant wishing to jump ship?

Growing up in abject poverty, seeing the lengths to which people would go to step over one another for the sake of putting food in their belly or dragging themselves out of the gutter, had triggered a fierce opposition against fathering a child. That had been long before his double rejection from both parents. *That* had merely cemented what he already knew. *Família* was a foolish illusion people wrapped themselves up in until the going got tough, then they were all too quick to throw off its burdens and disavow themselves from their responsibilities. As for that other worthless notion of familial love—?

The ringing of his silver phone shattered his bitter thoughts, and, with more than a little relief, he strode to his desk and snatched it up.

'Joao Oliviera,' he announced himself with the

power and authority that was second nature to him these days. Within minutes he'd returned to his natural habitat of proficient mogul with his eyes on the next challenging prize.

It was almost as if the last hour hadn't happened.

Except that it had.

Again, that noxious mix of imbalance and uncertainty welled inside him. It was an upsurge of memories of his past that was causing his disgruntlement, he concluded. And like every adversity, he'd conquer these, too.

With that firm assurance, he threw himself fully into his day.

When Saffie knocked and entered a few hours later, she too had returned to her rightful business mode. She was thoroughly up to speed with what his investigators had unearthed about Lavinia and put forward cogent ideas that perfectly augmented his own plans for the heiress.

By Wednesday morning the scene was set to step up the campaign to win over Lavinia Archer.

Joao had every intention of getting her to board the private jet he'd sent for her in South Africa. By midday he had his confirmation that she was on her way.

All it'd taken was a simple yet brilliant idea

from Saffron to send her a gold-embossed envelope containing nothing but the name of the renowned auction house in Shanghai.

For a jaded heiress like Lavinia Archer, the bait had been too much to resist.

It was a coup worth celebrating. He would have if his mood had improved since Monday. It hadn't.

So it was also a good thing Saffie had been out of the office at his stylist readying herself for their extended trip to Shanghai. For the last thirty-six hours he hadn't been able to glance at her without the aggravating reminder that she'd intended to walk away.

As a reminder to her of just how much she loved this job she'd been so eager to throw away, he'd set her endless tasks, at which she'd excelled. And yes, along the line, he'd been filled with a deep desire to watch her bone-deep composure crack.

Now he'd caught a glimpse of the fire that burned beneath her serene façade, he wanted to see more. Wanted to know what made her tick. So he wouldn't be taken by surprise again, he assured himself.

But deep down he knew it was more than that. This particular fire had been blazing since Morocco. Since the singular experience that came close only to the milestone years of turning his life around. Of making his first million.

It was the circumstances, he assured himself. The Archer deal consumed his life day and night. It was logical that everyone involved in it should take up space in his thoughts, too.

Lavinia.

Pueblo.

Saffie.

He swung away from where he'd been staring at the view.

The latest file on Pueblo needed to be read.

About to click on it, his fingers froze when warm, husky laughter reached his ears.

Saffie was out, and very few people were granted access to her office.

Rising and crossing his office, Joao pulled his door open and froze.

It was Saffie, chatting to another member of staff.

Mild shock pummelled him as he listened. He'd never heard Saffron like that before. Light. Airy. Friendly. *Utterly captivating.*

Utterly surprising, just as she'd surprised and captivated him in Marrakesh.

In what other ways was she different away from his sphere?

The need to delve deeper, uncover her secrets,

propelled him forward. 'Is this a private gathering or can I interrupt?'

She stiffened before swivelling around. The younger man looked equally startled. Joao took little satisfaction in his discomfort. He was still reeling over the latest facet of Saffie he'd just glimpsed.

'I got back a short while ago. My computer was frozen, so I got Andy from IT to take a look for me.'

'If he's done then perhaps normal service can resume?' he asked without taking his gaze from Saffie's flustered face.

Saffie barely nodded before Andy beat a hasty retreat.

'Did you have to do that?'

'Do what, exactly?'

'Talk to him that way. He was showing me pictures of his newborn niece.'

'He was wasting your time and therefore wasting mine. And I asked you to bring me the Hunter-Shrike file when you returned.'

'I put it on your desk two minutes after you asked for it. You were at your window staring at the view when I came in.'

Joao frowned. She'd been in his presence and he'd missed her? 'I was thinking.'

'About what?'

'About your little speech.'

She tensed, her eyes widening. 'What little speech?'

'Something along the lines of being a vampire who just takes and takes?'

Heat flowed into her cheeks. Joao rammed his hands in his pockets to resist the urge to trace the flow with his fingers. 'I didn't... I... Perhaps I could've phrased that better.'

'Only perhaps?'

Her lips pursed. 'So you were thinking about my speech...and?'

'You don't want a pay rise and you protest when I offer other incentives so I've decided to double the charitable donations I'll be making this year instead. We'll have a working dinner this evening and you can bring your list.'

'*My* list?'

He shrugged. 'You hurled the accusation, Saffie. You can help me become the better man.'

He returned to his office in a better mood.

Which lasted for a handful of hours, right until the moment his EA froze before the lift doors leading to his penthouse.

'Problem?' he asked, aware of the tension in his voice.

'Why are we having dinner in your...in the penthouse?'

'Because you left a notification in my diary that four of my ten departments are using every conference room and dining space for client mixers and would appreciate a ten-minute meet-and-greet if I had the chance? Did you forget, Saffie?'

She flushed. 'Oh... I... Yes, it slipped my mind.'

Joao held the lift door open as it went to close. 'Get in the lift, Saffie. I promise the only blood-red thing I'm after is the colour of my wine.'

She slanted an irritated glance at him. 'I'm not going to live that down, am I?'

A quiet satisfaction pulsed through him when she entered without protest. 'Likening your boss to a vampire? It's a subject I'm looking forward to discussing thoroughly at your next evaluation.'

She stared at him for several beats; blue eyes dark with apprehension and uncustomary uncertainty met his.

She sailed past him in heels that made her shapely legs seem endless. Her pinstriped dress tastefully followed her curves, with a zip that extended from her nape to the hem, and set his fingers tingling with torturous visions of him undressing her.

He took a sustaining breath as the lift doors glided shut.

Sim, they were swimming in uncharted waters. But it was a challenge he welcomed. Relished, even.

They exited into his penthouse and Saffie paused, her curious gaze flicking through the living room. It occurred to him that, despite their close working relationship, she'd only been up here a handful of times.

While work consumed a significant part of his life, he also relished the pleasures his lifestyle brought him. A helicopter on the roof of his building ensured he could be in any one of his four London or country residences within half an hour, entertaining clients or friends away from the office.

The setting sun slanted sultry light into the living room, directly onto the wide plush sofa, the orange glow uncomfortably reminiscent of a certain divan in Morocco.

Before he could halt it, memory returned full force, bombarding him with fiery blasts.

Gritting his teeth, he headed towards his dining room, relieved when his executive chef arrived minutes later and placed her dish of baby bok choy and noodle salad with shaved truffles in front of her, then returned with his chosen prime-cut Brazilian wagyu steak.

He picked up the bottle of red Chilean, a vintage from his personal vineyard, decanted and left to breathe by his chef, and frowned when Saffie shook her head.

'None for me, thanks. I have a headache.'

Like many things this week, that was a first. He redirected the crystal decanter to his own glass, aware he was frowning as he poured.

'Have you taken anything for it?'

She shrugged, although her gaze remained on her plate. 'I've been busy.'

He warmed his wine glass in his cupped hand. 'Too busy to take ten seconds out of your time to take care of yourself?'

She pushed a piece of bok choy around her plate before spearing it with a fork. 'Normally, it goes away by itself.'

He frowned. 'Normally?' he pressed, raising his glass to take a healthy mouthful. Something hot and heavy strummed inside him when her gaze fell to his mouth, then dropped to linger at his throat. She'd kissed him there that night in Morocco, he recalled a little too heatedly. Bit him, in fact.

'Why are you interested in my health issues, Joao?'

'This week you've accused me of working you to death or implied something just as unsavoury. So now I'm resolved to helping you get rid of your headache,' he countered, that dart of displeasure at drinking alone evaporating in the thrill of their banter.

'And you intend to do that by grilling me?'

'It's a good alternative to watching you push your dinner around your plate while you avoid my gaze.' Standing, he went to the sleek cabinet, took out the medical pouch stored there and brought back the tablets. 'Here.'

She set her silverware down in precise movements, lifted a pristine linen napkin to dab at her lips before accepting the mild headache pills.

Aggravatingly avoiding his gaze, she swallowed them. 'There, all sorted. Now shall we get off the subject?' she demanded in a tone far removed from her usual brisk delivery.

Joao settled back in his seat, forgoing the last bite of his excellent steak in favour of this discussion.

'Certainly,' he replied, his gaze clashing with eyes that were more grey than blue in the muted light of his private dining room. 'Did you bring your list? I'm aiming for you to think much better of me by week's end.'

She released her napkin with an abrupt toss, her face flaming. He curled his fingers tighter around his glass as the fierce desire to trace her cheek with his fingertips rammed deep.

'If you're trying to make me feel bad about what I said, don't bother,' she stated drolly.

He sipped and savoured another mouthful of wine. 'What if I mean it, Saffie? Will that make you…bend a little?'

Her eyes went wide. After a moment, she swallowed. 'I… I'm sure the charities in question will appreciate it.'

'I'm not talking about other charities. I'm asking about you.'

Her nostrils flared delicately as she took a long breath. The action expanded her ribcage, drawing his gaze to her full, heavy breasts. 'I guess that would be a start.'

'*Bem.* Let's do it.'

She eyed him a little warily, deepening his own questions about his motives. He already gave her far more than any other assistant. Was he really willing to go this far just to keep her?

Yes. Until his father was brought to heel, he would lasso the moon itself for her if required.

The little twinge that indicated his reasons weren't wholly altruistic, he chose to ignore, holding his hand out for the tablet.

He perused the list, noting that more than half were family and children-orientated. A different sort of twinge niggled him, one that forced him to consider whether she'd truly meant to leave him to chase flight dreams of babies and family.

Joao realised he was frowning when he handed the tablet back. 'Approved. You have my permission to gift each of them one hundred thousand pounds.'

Her lips parted in shock. 'That…that's too much.'

'I'm confident the organisations in question won't feel the same. Thank me and let's move on, Saffie.'

Her soft lips remained parted for another second, before her eyelashes swept down. 'Thank you, Joao,' she murmured huskily.

'*De nada.* What's next on the agenda?'

'Vincent Gingham is calling you in thirty minutes. Maybe we should—'

'Gingham can wait. You haven't had any dessert yet. I had Chef Bouillard prepare your favourite.' As if on cue, the Michelin-starred chef who travelled around the world with Joao and cooked almost every meal entered, holding aloft a silver platter. Joao nodded approvingly as he placed the dish in front of Saffron and retreated.

She eyed him suspiciously. 'What is it?'

He remained silent, watching her steadily. Her lips pursed again, then she lifted the cloche off the platter.

She inhaled sharply at the concoction before her. 'Joao, what are you doing?'

Not the response he'd been expecting. 'We are having a meal.'

She shook her head. 'Don't give me that. First that insanely expensive necklace. Now this?'

'It's dessert, Saffron. Let's not make a mountain and all that.'

'You said it was my favourite. A favourite thing is something you love and indulge in *occasionally*. This is a chocolate mousse topped with truffles and twenty-four-carat shaved edible gold. I've had it *once*, when you talked me into eating with you on New Year's Day.'

Joao shrugged. 'I thought you'd want to mark your continued employment with something you enjoyed. The necklace doesn't count. That's for the Archer deal, and was given before you enlightened me of your plans. Now eat up. Gingham is a bore when he's kept waiting inordinately.'

Saffron wouldn't exactly lower herself into glaring at him, but the look she sent him was close. Had he not still been caught up in alternate moments of surrealism and imbalance he would've smiled.

Instead he raised his glass, took another sip and watched Saffron dig her fork delicately into the gold and ochre creation, lift a mouthful to her lips, sneak a quick taste with the tip of her tongue before sliding it into her mouth.

He watched her suppress a moan and bit back one of his own as she gave a little shiver of pleasure.

Feeling the blood rush to his groin, he drained his glass and picked up his phone. He could've left her to it and returned to his office. But too many things had skidded off kilter this week. As absurd as it sounded, he wasn't in the mood to tempt fate by breaking this simple ritual of a working dinner.

Five long minutes later, he looked up at the delicate clatter of her fork on the plate.

'Thank you, Joao. That was amazing.'

He gave a brisk nod and stood, veering sharply away before her eyes dropped to the swell behind his fly. 'We'll have the meeting up here,' he said, heading for the door to his penthouse study. 'I want you on the Gingham videoconference. He behaves himself when you're present, and he definitely talks less bull.'

'You mean I reel him back when he goes off script?'

'Exactly.'

She nodded. 'I'll go and grab his file.'

Joao went to his desk, tugging off his tie and discarding it as he went. His casual attire would annoy the newspaper magnate from the Deep South but the great thing about the back-breaking climb to reach this pinnacle of success was that he was in an excellent position not to give a damn.

These days potential business partners needed him more than he needed them.

It hadn't always been the case, though...

He stilled, his fingers freezing against his shirt as memory crashed through him.

His mother screaming insults at him for deigning to be born.

Hunger the likes of which he wouldn't wish on his worst enemy.

A ruthless gang attempting to steal what little food he'd managed to scrounge from tourists.

The fight with one particularly vicious gang member that had nearly cost him a limb.

He unfurled his hand, stared at the scar that still tingled its reminder of that fateful night and the *favela* doctor who'd been his saviour.

'Joao? Is everything okay?'

He whirled around to face Saffron. Eyes that saw too much bore into him. '*Sim.* Everything's fine.' He freed his top button.

'Are you sure? Only you looked like—'

Her words strangled when he reached out, stroked his thumb over the corner of her upper lip. A delicate shiver raced through her, and her eyes darkened, right before she took a hasty step back.

'What are you doing?' she demanded huskily.

'Chocolate,' he stated abruptly, his own voice gruff and uneven. 'You have a tiny smear of chocolate on your lip. I don't think you want to take a video call wearing your dessert, do you?'

She exhaled. 'No. Uh…thanks.'

He brought his thumb to his lips, taking the time to lick and savour the delicacy and her taste.

Saffie made a tight, erotic little sound in her throat, one that punched through his resistance straight to the heart of forbidden desires.

Meu Deus.

He needed to move, turn away. Put some distance between them. But he couldn't. Worse still, he didn't want to.

Not when she was watching him with those wide blue eyes. Not when those lush lips called to him with siren-strong temptation.

She blinked, her nostrils quivering as she inhaled. 'Gingham…'

'We have ten minutes. More,' he rasped.

'I should…we should…'

Joao caught her to him, lust, hot and torrid and alarmingly strong, burning a blazing path through him.

What he was doing was terribly unwise. But he couldn't help himself.

He wrapped his arm tight around her slim waist and brought her flush against his body, his senses singing when she didn't resist.

Then, far too many weeks after that mild-altering first time, Joao fused his mouth to hers and tasted the woman who by all reason and logic should've remained untouchable.

CHAPTER FOUR

SAFFIE'S BODY WAS on fire, bypassing every shred of common sense to blaze in gloriously forbidden delight, even as her senses went to war with each other.

This wasn't supposed to happen.

Her every nerve ending shouldn't have awoken at that simple touch of his thumb on her mouth. Her breasts shouldn't have tingled in wild anticipation.

Joao wasn't supposed to drive her to the brink within seconds of kissing her. He wasn't supposed to use his hard, virile body to drive every thought from her head so easily…so masterfully.

And she…

Thoughts melted away as she strained against him, her mouth eagerly opening beneath his, craving more of the delirious pleasure that shouldn't have been flowing through her bloodstream.

A platonic three months.

No repeat of Morocco.

No loss of control.

And yet here she was, her every cell crying out in glee as Joao took complete and effortless control with just one touch. Every touch revving her senses into overdrive.

In her not too distant past, she'd been in a relationship that had lasted several months before it'd fizzled out and died a natural death.

Nothing she'd experienced then came close to what she'd felt with Joao in Marrakesh. Or the sensations he was evoking in her now.

Her breasts grew heavy and tingled as Joao pinned her against the glass wall in his study, propped her up with one muscular thigh between hers.

A thick, helpless moan spilled out of her.

They kissed with wild abandon that bordered on rabid. When the need for oxygen drove them apart, Joao stared down at her, his eyes blazing with hunger as desire arced between them, snapping and sizzling like forked lightning.

It was the same look he'd levelled at her that night in Marrakesh. The one that made her heart leap with frenzied anticipation, her core desperately needy with a hunger she'd never known before.

But there was also a hint of apprehension.

Because from the first moment she'd set eyes

on him, hadn't she sensed that he could wreak wicked sorcery on her senses? And hadn't that observation been conclusively proven two months ago?

Joao made a gruff sound under his breath, his hands sliding up her ribcage to boldly cup her breasts. Shamelessly, he moulded them as his kiss deepened, introducing an edge of hunger and possessiveness that robbed her of what little breath remained in her lungs.

When his fingers found the stiffened peaks of her nipples and mercilessly teased them, she shivered and strained into his touch with an eagerness bordering on abandon.

'Touch me, Saffie,' he grunted against her ear.

With a feverish little exhalation, she dragged her hands down his broad shoulders, over his chest to explore the hard planes of his stomach.

She barely felt the hem of her dress being lifted, the tops of her lace-stockinged thighs being exposed. But she certainly felt the heat of his fingers as they caressed her hip, revelled in the trail of fire as his fingers brushed the tops of her satin panties.

Joao's lips found hers again as his fingers delved beneath, seared her damp heat to stroke her core, began to explore her with expert skill that turned her knees liquid. That made her whimper.

He swallowed the sound, parted her, and—

Froze at the distinct tone of a videoconference summons ringing through the study.

Joao muttered something under his breath, the meaning lost between their lips as he plastered his masterful lips against hers once more.

The sound stopped for a moment before starting again.

Saffie blinked, barely managing to drag herself from the psychotropic effect of his kiss. 'Joao...'

'Ignore it, Saffie,' he growled.

But the icy brace of reality was sinking in deeper, reminding her where she was, what she was doing.

And with whom.

Dear God...

She pushed at his shoulders. 'No... Joao, stop.'

This time his curse was succinct, tossed out in sexy, pithy Portuguese. Against her belly, the thick evidence of his arousal pressed insistently, sharpening the hunger tearing through her.

He stepped back and whirled away, his fingers driving through his hair as he placed half the width of the room between them.

Saffie sucked in a desperate breath and frantically adjusted her dress as thick silence pounded through the room.

After a minute he glanced at her, one finger poised over the answer button. 'Are you ready?' he asked.

He was once again composed, master of all he surveyed, which was more or less the whole world, while she squirmed in the pit of unfulfilled desire.

But Saffie managed to nod, managed to drag herself into the chair next to Joao with her tablet poised before her as the screen flicked to life.

And when they were done and Joao had effortlessly hammered another deal, she scrambled to her feet. 'I'm going back to the office. I have a million things to do before we fly tomorrow afternoon.'

She told herself she was thankful that he barely glanced up from the file. That when he replied, 'Very well. I'll be down in ten,' his tone was once again cool and indifferent.

It was what she needed to keep her from falling for temptation again.

So why did it bruise her heart so badly?

Exiting the penthouse, Saffie wrestled quaking fingers into functionality long enough to summon the lift and stumble into it, before her legs gave way and she sagged against the polished mirror, her breaths coming in frantic little pants.

Dear God…

The way he'd commanded her body. The way she'd thrilled to all of it.

She swallowed, feeling another fierce blush heat up her face as her hand went to her throat, caressing the skin as if it would soothe the rawness that echoed in her head from her loss of control.

She'd fallen into each caress, each kiss, like a sex-starved lover, eagerly welcoming her paramour, offering herself to him on a silver platter.

Her breath shook out.

She had no business experiencing the awe trawling through her. Not when she'd finally understood over the past two days just how much the Archer deal meant to him. Not when she now suspected the reason for the absence of a new lover in his life stemmed from his zeal to win the Archer deal.

So, she could've been any of the supermodels or socialites he usually dated, a way to slake his needs without the tedium of wining and dining a new paramour.

Just like that night in Marrakesh, she'd been there, available and willing. Simply a warm body gracing his bed until he worked her out of his system while ensuring she stayed put to play her part in his business deal.

The thought tossed a cold wave at her, restoring a little of her shattered equilibrium.

From the start, Joao had represented a heady but *temporary* thrill. She just needed to remind herself of that, perhaps a little more forcefully and constantly so this feeling of transcendence, this foolish quaking of her heart would cease.

Despite the admonition, heat rushed to her core in remembrance of how he'd touched her, her belly clenching with cloying hunger.

Desperately suppressing it, she threw herself into the last items on her to-do list.

By the time Joao came downstairs she was at her desk. She sensed him prowling his office, her awareness of him almost superhuman as her frayed senses refused to settle.

'You didn't tell me how the session with the stylist went.'

She jumped, unaware he'd been standing in the doorway.

Whisky-dark eyes surveyed her with deceptively lazy focus, the espresso cup held between long, tapered fingers.

The dark trousers and burgundy shirt he wore highlighted his superb musculature. A warm, tight body she'd explored less than an hour ago.

Saffie's pulse tripped and she scrambled to think straight. Then decided against pointing out that their conversation when she'd returned from her outing had been anything but affable. Or that he'd never shown an interest in her stylist sessions before today. 'It went fine. No hiccups,' she said briskly.

His jaw clenched for a taut moment before he nodded. *'Bom.'*

He remained in the doorway. And, unwitting fool that she was, Saffie's gaze flicked to his. She attempted to read his expression. Felt her stomach drop when she read nothing but neutral, professional interest.

As silently as he'd appeared, Joao retreated.

And then proceeded to make demand after impatient demand, as if determined to recoup every minute of the time they'd spent in that illicit embrace.

For the first time in her life, Saffie found herself clock-watching. And grabbing her bag the moment the clock struck nine.

He had the phone to his ear when she poked her head through the door, although those piercing eyes locked on her and narrowed as she indicated she was leaving. When he made to pause the conversation, Saffie waved him away.

And fled.

On a wild whim, she instructed the personal driver Joao had hired for her to take her home to Chiswick.

She'd bought her flat two years ago, mostly to invest her more than generous salary. Her frantically busy role as Joao's EA meant she got to stay in her flat once or twice a week if she was lucky. Half of the plants she kept defiantly buying because she expected her life to miraculously slow down survived only because her next-door neighbour took pity and watered them when he could.

The majority of what little down time she got was spent in one of the executive condos Oliviera Enterprises kept for its high-ranking employees. It was where she kept her work clothes, where she'd crashed in the early hours of yesterday morning after working with Joao for sixteen hours straight on the top ten deals he was juggling.

And now, as she walked around rooms that should've felt familiar but didn't, Saffie's mind was back in the penthouse. Back against that glass wall, her senses clamouring for everything Joao had to give.

How she wanted to be back there now, caution be damned.

With grim determination she pulled out her

suitcase and gathered the few essentials she kept at the flat. It struck her that she could walk out of her flat and never return because everything she needed was taken care of at the company's executive suite.

The awareness that she had allowed herself to become fully dependent on Joao sent a pulse of apprehension through her. She shook free of it a moment later.

She'd pulled herself back from falling into total disgrace after vowing to keep away from her powerful, charismatic boss today. She was allowed a few wobbly moments.

Order would be restored tomorrow.

Except it wasn't.

Joao's bad mood arrived, and stayed, displaying a full spectrum of his Latin temper that sent her assistants cowering. Eventually, knowing Joao would be locked in meetings and conference calls in the hours before they flew to Shanghai, she gave them permission to leave mid-afternoon.

With the videoconference she'd set up for him about to commence, Saffie decided to make herself scarce, too.

She was eager to flee her thoughts, but more than that she was eager to shake off the addictive hunger that had taken root inside her and wouldn't shift.

Standing up from her desk, she started as the intercom buzzed to life.

With unsteady fingers, she answered. 'Yes?'

'Come into my office, please, Saffie,' Joao commanded.

She replaced the handset, feverishly making a list of what he could possibly want and abandoning it after a few seconds. Joao's needs were fluid and numerous.

Thoughts of needs immediately intensified her hunger, thickening the vein of desire he'd effortlessly triggered in her. Desire he'd more than fulfilled in Morocco only for it to return ten times stronger.

Her footsteps faltered outside his doors despite her traitorous senses yearning for the man within.

She slicked unusually clammy hands down her merino-wool-clad thighs. She worked for the man and knew it wasn't her overactive imagination broadcasting his impatience from behind the closed doors.

And when she opened those doors she wasn't fooled for a second by his seemingly relaxed pose behind his desk.

Fiercely intent eyes latched on her the moment

she stepped inside and tracked her mercilessly across the plush carpet.

'What do you need?' she asked in a voice nowhere near her usual even tones.

He stared at her for a terse few seconds before he flicked a glance at his watch. 'The Silverton team weren't ready with their report. They're under orders to get themselves into shape and reconvene for the videoconference in half an hour.'

She frowned. 'I spoke to them this morning. We went through the bullet points and everything was in place. I wouldn't have arranged the meeting otherwise.' She'd learned to her advantage that triple-checking those with access to Joao was better for everyone concerned, including her.

He pushed back his chair and rose. 'They weren't ready to my satisfaction. So we have fifteen minutes. Correction, we *had* fifteen minutes. Since you wasted five minutes with your dawdling, now we have ten,' he drawled as he rounded his desk.

The swift spike of excitement robbed her of breath and immediately replaced it with a racing heart and shrieking warning that this... *anticipation* coursing through her was skating dangerously close to foolhardy. 'Ten minutes for what?'

He raised one mocking eyebrow. 'To discuss what happened yesterday. Specifically, if it's going to cause another episode like Monday's.'

Her heart flipped in her chest. 'Why should it?'

'You tell me. I would've had this conversation with you last night, but you made yourself rather…unavailable.'

She couldn't hide the blush that suffused her face. 'I went home. To my flat,' she added for emphasis she wasn't altogether sure was necessary. 'As for dissecting what happened…there's no need.'

His eyes narrowed as he rounded his desk to perch on the edge. Her pulse skipped erratically at the sight of his thighs bunching beneath his tailored trousers.

'Are you sure?'

'Absolutely. Let's chalk it under a lapse of judgement.'

His lips compressed and his nostrils thinned as he inhaled. 'How magnanimous of you,' he drawled.

Dragging her gaze from the enthralling sight, she cleared her throat. 'If there's nothing else, I have a meeting in three minutes.'

He scowled. 'What meeting?'

'The executive assistants' meeting. It's scheduled in sync with your call.'

'Cancel it,' he growled.

She shook her head. 'I've cancelled it three times already. As head of the executives I can't not turn up.'

For the longest time, he didn't answer, his eyes lingering on her. Then abruptly he stood and returned to his desk.

Saffie started to walk away but then paused. 'Joao?'

'Hmm?' His gaze was hooded as it lingered on her.

'Were the Silverton team really not ready?'

A look very much like chagrin flashed across his face. 'They spent too long trying to get the projector to start the presentation. I grew impatient.'

'By too long, you mean ten seconds, possibly less?'

He clawed his fingers through his dishevelled hair. The action was so sexy, she forced her gaze away before she made a fool of herself by drooling. 'Perhaps. The other reason I wanted you in here is because I want your input on Silverton. He's hiding something, I'm not exactly sure what. But, of course, if you need to attend your meeting...'

Slowly, Saffie retraced her steps. Leaning forward, she picked up his phone and dialled the familiar number. 'Hello, Mr Oliviera?'

'No, Justine, it's Saffie. Something's come up. I won't make the meeting. No, don't cancel it. You can take it for me. Send me the notes when you're done.'

'Oh. Okay. If you're sure?'

'I'm sure. Thanks.'

She hung up and met Joao's gaze. 'There. That's taken care of.'

Whisky-gold eyes stayed locked on hers for a long moment then an expression crossed his face. It was hard. Bitter. Enough to make her stomach tense. *'Obrigado.'*

'What exactly do you want me to watch out for?' she asked, desperate to stop her mind from searching for reasons behind that look.

'I'm not sure, but, whatever it is, I will get to the bottom of it.' The grit coating the words made her wonder if he referred to something other than the Silverton meeting.

As had been happening far too often lately, her mind began to stretch, yearning for knowledge she wasn't entitled to. A need to know the man beneath the outer dynamism and authority.

Why did she sometimes find him staring at the scar in his palm with a mixture of anguish and poignancy? Why did he always close his fist as if holding a precious memory close?

She glanced up and caught him staring at her, a puzzling expression on his face.

'What?'

'I think the Silverton team are ready for us now,' he said with a touch of brittle amusement.

Her startled gaze dropped to the ringing phone. Face flaming, she snatched it up. 'Oliviera Enterprises. Of course, Mr Silverton. I'll let him know you're ready for him.'

She hit the mute button. Without glancing at Joao, she pressed the button that lowered the videoconferencing screen.

When she chanced a glance at him again, the bitterness had receded, and he was once again the all-powerful billionaire.

While she was evolving into an unfocused mess.

She swallowed, vowing to restore her composure by hell or high water, as the screen flickered to life.

'You're better prepared now, I trust?' Joao drawled.

Rick Silverton nodded almost fawningly. 'Of course, sir. And apologies for the earlier glitch.'

Joao waved him away. 'I am confident you

will ensure it doesn't happen again. Now, your report, please. Then the projections.'

Saffie wasn't sure what made her glance at Joao then. His eyes were firmly fixed on her. And the look in them sent a different kind of sensation down her spine. The one that warned she'd just skated closer to the edge of the volcano.

They took off from a private airport in South London four hours later. Any one of the four bedrooms in the converted A320 Airbus's vast, jaw-droppingly luxurious interior would've been a perfect place to regroup after a very charged seventy-two hours.

Except her boss had other ideas and none of them included giving Saffie a moment to herself.

Five minutes after take-off, Joao beckoned her to the sumptuous chocolate-leather-and-mahogany-themed conference room that also served as his study on board. On two large screens, several Oliviera Enterprise executives from New York and India were poised to give an update on several projects.

That ate up three hours.

The moment they were done, Joao swivelled in his armchair to face her. He didn't speak immediately, an unsettling tactic that had failed to rattle her until recently. Until she'd become intimately acquainted with her boss one night in Morocco and now couldn't look at any part of his body without recalling in vivid detail what it felt like to be up close against his warm, vibrant skin. To experience the unleashed power of his masculinity. To remember the feel of those sensual lips suckling her nipple, wreaking dark magic between her thighs.

Enough!

It was clear he intended to throw her off-balance, probably because of yesterday's rebellion of leaving the office while he was on the phone. Well, he could try all he wanted.

Saffie cleared her throat. 'Mrs Archer landed in Shanghai two hours ago. I have it on good authority, she's thrilled with her suite and the presents we arranged for her.'

'*You* arranged. Feel free to take credit where it's due.' The suggestion was delivered in a laconic rasp, his eyes leaving hers to trail lazily over her body, his eyes heating where they touched on her tasteful soft beige trousers and blush-pink off-the-shoulder cashmere top.

Too unnerved to look into those eyes just yet, she pulled her tablet closer.

'We'll have dinner with her at her favourite restaurant two hours after we land. Chef Bouillard has been given exclusive charge of the kitchen for one night and been apprised of her culinary preferences. But I've suggested he delight her with a few of his own signature dishes. Same old, same old won't impress her.'

'My sentiments exactly.'

She nodded. 'Two more bidders have joined the private auction for the Shanzi orchid. That brings the total to eleven. Sadly, the auctioneers couldn't be persuaded to keep it at nine.'

One eyebrow rose. 'Are you losing your touch, Saffie?' he mused.

'It's more like word has leaked that you're interested and that's attracted the usual upstarts who think they can beat you on any arena,' she replied, then realised how sycophantic she sounded.

A quick glance showed a wider, more arrogant smile that irritatingly made her stomach dip in excitement. He rose from his seat, ventured closer until his scent reached out and wrapped around her. Saffie kept her gaze trained on her tablet, cautioning herself not to do anything stupid, like look into those compelling eyes. Or trace the back of the large hand that landed on the table next to hers as he leaned down to peruse the list on her tablet.

'It is of no consequence. I intend to win at all costs,' he rasped low and deep.

She shivered, unsure whether he meant the auction specifically or the Archer deal.

Winning was everything to him. And yet, something in his demeanour blared alarm to her brain. One she couldn't decipher when he stood this close to her. When she felt as if he could hear her every heartbeat.

She really needed to get herself together.

She pulled up the next item on the agenda. 'The investigators sent the latest report on Pueblo Oliviera.'

The hand next to hers curled on the table and a different sort of tension seized his frame. This time, Saffie couldn't stop herself from looking up.

A hard, cynical mask stared back at her. But this close, within the depths of his eyes she saw something else. Ferocious, supremely intimate purpose. The kind birthed through whispered vows made in chilling darkness. The kind she'd made to herself when despair had held her in its tightest grip. When deepest yearnings had risen to the fore and threatened to consume her alive.

It was on one of those dark nights that she'd sworn she would never remain alone, that she would fulfil her promise to her foster mother and surround herself with a family, even if it was a family of two, and put the desolate solitude and heartache she'd suffered as a child behind her.

Pueblo Oliviera.

Even though she'd suspected, she'd never asked Joao for confirmation. From the naked flames leaping in his eyes, now wasn't a good time either.

And yet…a small voice called to her, urged her to probe.

'He's your father, isn't he?'

'A biological donor I had the dubious honour of being named after, *sim*,' he replied with a harsh rasp.

She'd done an Internet search early on in her role when she'd spotted the confidential memos on the man. Pueblo was rich and influential. Nowhere in his son's league, of course, but with enough clout in the business world to go after the same deals Joao did.

It hadn't taken long to recognise the brutal rivalry between the two men. Rivalry that went beyond mutual business interests.

'Do you two speak?'

He laughed bitterly. '*Sim*, we do. Through the profit-and-loss score board. Specifically, my profits, his losses.'

'Why?' She didn't need to elaborate.

His eyes hardened and she held her breath,

afraid she'd overstepped. She was about to excuse herself when he straightened abruptly and strolled to the elaborate drinks bar set into the side of one sleek table. He poured himself a shot of Hardy L'Ete Lalique champagne cognac that Saffie knew cost more than most people's monthly salaries. In another glass, he poured mineral water and returned to the desk. She took the glass and set it down, too frazzled to drink.

He downed his in one go, and slid the glass onto the polished table.

'My birth was a mistake. One he wasn't prepared to acknowledge. So, let's just say I've made it my business to remain in his crosshairs.'

She gasped. 'He said that to you? That you were a mistake?'

Hooded eyes met hers before he shrugged. 'In certain circumstances, words aren't needed. A child is aware of how its parents feel about him without vocal expression. It's not a failing to admit you're not ready for fatherhood and take steps to prevent it. I know that for myself. It is a shame he didn't.'

A tight hollow pushed against her diaphragm, making it agonising to breathe. 'You don't want children?' she asked through numb lips, seeking clarification despite everything she'd learned about him pointing to this.

He didn't answer for the longest time. A stretch of time when something shrivelled inside her.

Eventually he shrugged. 'It's not a goal I've set for myself. Pueblo could've walked away from his mistake, instead he set out to make himself my enemy. It's been…infinitely amusing to lock horns with him.'

'You don't look particularly amused,' she replied, throwing herself back into the conversation so she wouldn't have to examine why her heart mourned.

'*Não*, not this time. Because he's got it into his head that he can steal the Archer deal from under my nose.'

'That's why you're so determined to win, isn't it? Because he's your main opposition?'

'You forget that I'm first and foremost a businessman. And this is the most lucrative deal to cross my desk in a few years.'

Despite the reminder, Saffie knew that wasn't all. Joao intended to beat his father at the highest level, once and for all.

Why? What exactly had happened between father and son?

Self-preservation rattled its warning again. She glanced at his set features and knew it was time to exercise discretion. To curb that growing need to dig beneath the wildly successful mogul to the man who…what?

Held the world in the palm of his hands with wizard-like ease that secretly fascinated her more and more with each passing day?

What good would come of knowing him?

They would never be in the same league.

For the next three months she would live on the edge with him. But after that—

She stepped away from the bleak picture stretching in her mind's eye. She'd been up for…goodness, she couldn't even remember. She needed to finish this task and head to bed. But before she could continue, he spoke.

'Do you think less of me, Saffie?' he asked abruptly.

'What?'

'Given the choice, would you not pay your own mother back for abandoning you? For leaving you to be cared for by strangers?'

Her breath shrivelled in her lungs. 'You know that I grew up in a care home?'

'*Sim.* You know enough about my life. Seems fair I knew about yours.'

She took a minute to absorb the news, to will calm into her racing heart. 'I have questions, of course I do. But until I hear her side of the story, I don't know what I would've done.'

'But you must have imagined a scenario of some sort?' he pressed, making her wonder if he'd done the same and been met with disappointment. Was that what had turned him bitter?

She shrugged. 'I've been through every emotion you can think of. But when it comes down to it, I simply don't know why she did what she did. And…somehow I've learned to live with it. To be thankful for the time I had with my foster mother.'

His lips pursed and his eyes probed as if he was attempting to see beneath her words.

Unwilling to unmask the depth of her loneliness, she shifted her attention back to business. 'Would you like me to read the report?' she asked.

He shrugged. 'Let's hear it.'

She clicked on the document, perused the list of Pueblo's activities in the past month. 'His business dealings in Qatar are up for renegotiation next month. There's a bid for six wineries in South Africa. An Italian cargo haulage firm has approached him about merging.'

'I want the names of the parties in the Qatar deal. The rest he can keep. What else?'

She swallowed, a tad apprehensive about mentioning the final item. 'Lavinia Archer has an appointment with him next Monday in San Francisco.'

His smile was chilling. 'She won't be taking that meeting.'

The sheer arrogance of that statement was thrilling and frightening. 'May I ask why you're so confident?'

He sauntered around the table, sure and agile, self-assured and, oh, so sexy. 'Because *we* will be making plans to take Lavinia to Brazil.'

'But… Brazil wasn't on the agenda.'

Joao tugged the tablet out of her nerveless hands, tossed it on the table before drawing her chair firmly back from the conference table. 'It wasn't five minutes ago. Now it is.'

With a neat little flick of his hand, he swivelled her to face him. The solid column of his body threatened to trip her senses. 'I… Okay. Would you like me to—?'

'I think I've slave-driven you enough for one day. I'm not inclined to give you another excuse for a repeat of Monday's performance.'

His fingers tightened over the leather and Saffie couldn't look away from his hands. It was almost as if he held her. Heat flooded through her system, concentrating between her legs with a vivid insistence that made her stomach clench. 'In that case, I think we should head to bed.'

His gaze grew hot and hooded, his hands sliding down the side of the chair, drawing inexorably closer to where her arms rested on the cushion. 'Or…at least, I should,' she clarified hastily.

'Ah, *sim*. Your fragile humanity is rearing its head again? I believe this is where my supposed immortality dictates I should press on?' he rasped in deep, sexy tones.

Saffie flushed, angled her body away from him and hopped to her feet. When she'd put a few much-needed feet between them, she cleared her throat. 'Are you incapable of letting anything go?'

A peculiar light intensified the gold in his eyes. 'Apparently not.'

'If you expect me to apologise—'

His lips parted, the hint of a rare smile lightening his features, throwing her insides into chaos. 'And miss the chance to hold it over your head for the foreseeable future? Why would I do that?'

Saffie shook her head, more to clear it than anything else. 'You should go to bed. We need to sync our body clocks with Shanghai time.'

Whisky-gold eyes narrowed. 'You're also uncharacteristically skittish. Would you care to explain why?'

'Perhaps because I'm exhausted?'

He moved towards her. When his hands descended on either side of her hips, and he leaned in, she stopped breathing. 'You thrive on the work I give you, Saffie. This is something else.'

A shower of shivers rained over her as his gaze pinned her in place. 'It's nothing but exhaustion. Now, if you don't mind?'

'I do mind. You're not planning on another skirmish, are you? Because I warn you, my patience isn't infinite.'

She barely stopped herself from snorting. 'Tell me about it,' she said under her breath. He heard it. And grasped her chin to tilt her gaze to his. When she met his eyes, there was a hard glint within, one that sent awareness racing down her spine. For the longest time, he stared, hard and deep, probing beneath her skin.

'It's too late for regrets, Saffie. I hope you're aware of this and don't intend to disappoint me by reneging.'

At this point she feared it would be as impossible as cutting off her arm. 'No, I'm not.'

A curious tension eased out of him and, for a flash of time, she wondered if he felt the same as her.

With a shake of her head, she dismissed the absurd notion. His ultimate goal was the Archer deal. Everything else, including her brief sojourn in his bed, was a pleasant extra.

'*Bom*, as long as we're on the same page.'

'Now that's settled, I'm going to bed. If you need me let me know.'

His gaze rushed over her face, settling on her mouth with a ferocity that made it tingle. When that tingle arrowed south, she knew it was time to go.

His lips firmed. 'I'm not a complete tyrant. I'm sure I'll manage without you for a few hours while you rest.'

'Okay…well, I'll set my alarm to wake up a couple of hours before we land.'

He nodded, abruptly dismissing her.

On legs that felt weirdly reluctant to carry her forward, she walked to the door.

'Saffie?'

She froze, held onto the door handle for dear life. 'Yes?'

'Sleep well.'

Her sleeveless red-sequinned gown followed the contours of her body before dropping dramatically to trail on the floor behind her. Saffie wasn't sure why she'd let the stylist talk her into this outfit. It was by far the most exquisite piece of couture she owned.

The only problem was she'd never worn anything so…*red* or so bold in her life. To pick now, with her senses in deep disarray—when every cell in her body felt as if it were going to turn itself inside out every time Joao got within touching distance—felt like one challenge too many.

She examined herself more closely and breathed a little easier that the faint shadows she'd woken up with just before they'd landed were hidden beneath expensive concealer. The gown projected the confidence she needed. The kind of sophistication Joao Oliviera exuded so effortlessly and expected those in his sphere to emulate, no matter how much they wanted to lock themselves in a hotel room and hide from their perplexing emotions.

Therefore, she was suitable for purpose. Especially tonight, when the first charm offensive to win over Lavinia Archer needed to go off without a hitch.

She stepped away from the mirror.

There was no hiding from this.

Accepting that she couldn't go back on the promise she'd made to stay had been easy. What had caused her to toss and turn on the sumptuous king-size bed on Joao's jet was how quickly the composure she'd been sure would hold for the next three months seemed to careen out of control.

It was reassuring that whatever was ailing her emotions hadn't affected her professional performance.

The fact that her spirits remained flat despite that small comfort she chose to put down to jet lag. She was repeating that to herself when a hard rap shattered the silence in her suite.

The walk across the vast floor of the Sky Suite of the Shanghai Reign Hotel, the top half of the seven-star skyscraper hotel exclusively reserved for individuals with billionaire status, gave her time to take a few composure-restoring breaths.

Which proved pathetically useless when she opened the double doors and caught a glimpse of Joao.

She'd seen him in a tuxedo countless times.

But there was an indefinable, utterly mesmerising layer of magnificence that reached into her chest and squeezed the oxygen from her lungs. She couldn't fight the sly little voice that suggested it was that intimacy she feared that was creating havoc with her senses.

His hair gleamed under the soft lights of the private marble-floored foyer, his razor-sharp cheekbones shadowed as he leaned forward slightly and perused her from head to toe.

She held her breath, unsure whether she wanted him to comment on her appearance or remain aloofly impersonal. What she received was a slow stiffening of his body, a tightness to his jaw that sent a shiver down her spine.

'Something wrong?' she asked with a tremor in her voice that drew an inward grimace.

He didn't answer, merely conducted a return journey, slower this time until his glinting, blistering gaze clashed with hers.

'Voce parece sublime.' The words were growled out, as if they annoyed him.

'I only caught the last word.' And unless she was mistaken, it'd been a compliment, albeit a curt one. Her heart flipped, then began an insistent banging against her ribs.

'Then perhaps you should learn Portuguese, Saffie. With your brilliant abilities I'm surprised you haven't done so already.'

She was leaving in a few short months. What would be the point? The sharp prickle in her chest robbed her of her next breath but she powered through it. 'Since you speak impeccable English, I didn't see the need to prioritise it. Are you going to translate what you just said?'

Burnished gold eyes clashed with hers. 'That can be your first translation lesson.' Tension eased out of him, his powerful body assuming another, equally skin-tingling stance. The kind that heightened her awareness of his sheer animal masculinity. The kind that made her breath shorten even further and flung the sharpest arrows of lust to her sex.

'Did you…did you want something, Joao?' Why did his name have to leave her lips with such throaty emphasis?

His gaze dropped to her neck. 'I thought you might appreciate help with your necklace.'

The diamond and ruby necklace he'd given her on Monday. The day she'd announced she was going to leave him. The day he'd told her he needed her…

Had that been four short days ago?

'Oh. I was saving it for another occasion.' Like a summons to Buckingham Palace, which might hopefully never come.

His gaze lingered at her throat, then dropped down to her dress. 'Did you not pick this dress with the necklace in mind?'

He caught her slight grimace. 'What's the problem?'

'I still think it's a little too much.'

'I don't care what people think. You shouldn't either, Saffie. Either wear it or don't. Your choice.'

His lips firmed before he glanced pointedly

at the one-of-a-kind Richard Mille watch on his wrist. The timepiece came with a staggering price of two million dollars, and had been a gift, an astute move that had seen the iconic Swiss watchmaker's profits soar after Joao had been seen wearing it. 'Either way, we're stretching the limits of being fashionably late.'

Now he was leaving the decision to her, she admitted reluctantly, the gown was the perfect foil for the breathtaking necklace.

She crossed the room, the feast of wealth and opulence all around her in the form of gold-leaf-embossed cabinetry, expensive suede sofas, Tiffany lamps and a fringed waterfall chandelier made of Swarovski crystals and flawless tanzanite, paling in comparison to Joao, who followed her to the thumb-printed safe set behind a French Impressionist painting.

She took out the necklace and held it out to him.

He looked from the necklace to her throat. 'Turn around,' he instructed a little gruffly.

Struggling to take one more breath, Saffie turned. He stepped close, enough for the suppressed power of his presence to engulf her like an expensive cloak. For her body to tremble when he brushed up against her back.

She squeezed her eyes shut, praying for better

composure as the cool, heavy weight of price-less diamonds and rubies encircled her neck. She didn't need the mirror to know it would be dazzling, and Joao's satisfied nod when he caught her shoulders and spun her around to face him was sign enough that she'd passed his elegance test.

'Perfeita,' he murmured.

The warm glow the compliment sparked stayed with her long after they were ensconced in the back of a gleaming Rolls-Royce Phantom, the bodyguards Joao never travelled without in two SUVs in front and behind them as they travelled along the Bund towards their destination in Pudong.

He remained rigidly courteous as they alighted in front of the vaunted House of Pearls auction house twenty minutes later. The hosts of the event, dressed in sharp suits, fell over themselves to greet Joao, ushering them inside the hallowed red-carpeted room where the pre-auction champagne reception was being held.

Lavinia Archer was the first to spot Joao.

The septuagenarian, dressed in a stunning dove-grey gown and a haphazard combination of diamonds and pearls, smiled as they approached.

'You're a wicked one, Oliviera. Tempting me

with that little puzzle you knew I wouldn't be able to resist.'

He took her hand, placed a charming kiss on the back of it, before smiling. 'I insist you call me Joao, and I'm glad my ruse worked but the credit must go to my executive assistant. You remember Saffron?'

Now she knew a little of his history, Saffie suspected her invitation to call him by his first name stemmed from not wanting anything in common with the man who'd sired him. What other demons lay beneath his smooth surface?

As if he'd caught her question, his sharp gaze flicked to her, and narrowed.

'Of course.' Lavinia turned to Saffie and gasped. 'Goodness, what a fabulous necklace! It looks simply divine on you. Whatever you did to earn that, my dear, take my advice and keep doing it.'

Saffie tensed, and, although Lavinia's tone was more generous awe than maliciously salacious, the blood froze in her veins.

Before Morocco comments like that would've bounced off her skin. After all, working for the richest man in the world came with the guarantee that the eyes of the world would be on her twenty-four-seven. So why were her insides churning now? Was she broadcasting her inability to think straight around the man?

Hysteria bubbled up her throat.

'What's wrong?' Joao asked from beside her.

Frantically, she shook her head. 'Nothing.'

His eyes narrowed, a disappointed gleam lighting the depths. 'You've always spoken your mind to me, Saffie. Don't start hiding now.'

But how could she tell him how exposed she felt? How one night with him had turned her emotions inside out so that she couldn't even recognise them any more?

She glanced away from him, relief seeping into her when they were led from the reception room to the auction room. She was further saved from examining her feelings as a familiar, smiling face approached.

William Ashby III. The man who'd tried to poach her countless times in the past until she'd finally hinted that she might be in the market for a job soon. As with all things Will, he'd responded to her email on Monday to say she wouldn't be accepting his job offer after all with cheerful charm.

Lanky, congenial and fair-headed with a work-less-play-harder ethic, he was as different from Joao as night from day. An English aristocrat with a few billion to his name, Will by his own admission did just enough to keep his company's balance sheets in the black and spent the rest of his time chasing material highs.

And attempting to headhunt Saffie whenever they met.

'I thought that was you,' he said with a wide, boyish smile.

'Hello, Will.'

His smile widened. 'Almost didn't recognise you over the sparkle of that bling,' he teased.

Self-consciously, her hand went to the necklace, excuses rising and then dying on her lips as she concluded that she didn't owe anyone an explanation for Joao's generosity. Her chin rose and something in her expression made Will's eyebrow spike.

'I thoroughly approve of that fierce look, Saffie. Enough to make me throw caution to the wind and say I'll double whatever Oliviera's paying you if you change your mind and come work for me.'

Saffron smiled for the first time in a while. 'Just double? I'll have you know I received an offer just this week to triple it. An offer I refused.'

'Ouch.' He clutched his chest and gave a booming laugh that attracted interested gazes.

Including Joao's chilling look of disapproval,

which stayed on her for several heartbeats before it swung to Will. There it intensified, a combative gleam filming his eyes.

'Oops, I think I've stepped right into your boss's crosshairs. Should I be terrified?' Will's tone was amused with a trace of speculation.

'Maybe,' she teased. 'He knows about your job offer,' she explained, dragging her gaze from Joao.

Will stared down at her, his eyes twinkling. 'Dear God, did you feed me to the lion without as much as a heads up?'

She bit her tongue, unwilling to divulge the circumstances surrounding why his name had come up.

Will was still staring at her when Joao approached them, his prowl animalistic and irritatingly hypnotic.

'Ashby,' he greeted him with icy curtness.

'Oliviera, you caught me attempting to poach your assistant again,' Will said without a trace of apology.

'So I see. Perhaps it's time for me to stake my claim once and for all,' Joao replied, his narrowed gaze holding a chilling challenge that slowly dimmed Will's smile. Without giving the man a chance to respond, he turned darkly gleaming whisky-gold eyes on her. 'Do you think that would be necessary, Saffie?'

Her mouth dried because she knew they weren't talking about work any more. They'd strayed into something brutally personal. Something spell-binding and exhilarating. Something that made her breasts tingle and swell, made her pulse heat up and her feminine core clench with unashamed need.

'That won't be necessary. Will knows where he stands,' she said a little too hurriedly.

Will's shrewd gaze swung between her and Joao. Then he smiled and nodded. 'Indeed I do. Enjoy the rest of the evening.'

He walked away with a brisker stride than she'd ever seem him adopt, leaving her with an intensely brooding Joao.

'If I didn't know better, I'd say you encourage him in his erroneous beliefs,' he slanted at her.

He was understandably disgruntled. Normally she would have circumnavigated it by tactfully changing the subject. And considering she'd spent her life tempering her emotions, squash-ing her hurt and sorrow in the hopes that her prayers would be answered, that she would be picked next time and her desolation and loneli-ness would end, she should've been able to mask it now.

But for some unfathomable reason, Saffie didn't want to. She wanted to stamp her feet and shout that this was supposed to be an enjoyable experience. A thrilling swansong to end all swansongs before she swapped the roller coaster for what her heart yearned for most.

Joao had never demanded that she temper herself. She'd chosen that path because it was what had served her well in the past.

So why now? Why the urge to flex her emotions, take a leaf from his Latin temperament book and *let go*, just this once?

Because that's how Morocco happened!

The bracing reminder made her clutch the glass of champagne she'd barely sipped tighter. 'Well, I don't. But I think we need to talk when... when we get back to the hotel.'

'No,' he replied succinctly.

'What? You don't even know—'

'Don't I? You've been squirming your way to this since yesterday.'

'I don't squirm.'

His smile was tight and taunting. 'You didn't before Monday. But the past few days have been enlightening for both of us, haven't they, Saffie?'

Her insides flipped. 'I...don't know what you mean.'

'No? Well, let me speak for myself, then. It's

been eye-opening to see the woman beneath the cool exterior. To feel the passion beneath all that rigid efficiency.'

Her face flamed. That extremely masculine smile widened. 'It's too late to put the genie back in the bottle, Saffie. Whatever the outcome, I won't allow you to scurry back to prim placidity.'

She opened her mouth, but an usher was heading towards them, the front seats reserved for them ready and waiting.

Saffie was forced to swallow her response as the room hushed and they rejoined Lavinia.

Joao stayed firmly beside her as the auctioneer stepped up to the podium. 'As we all know, this isn't a run-of-the-mill auction. Occasions like these only come around once in a blue moon. Tonight, we're extremely honoured to have such an esteemed gathering here to witness the unveiling of the Shanzi orchid. This eight-year-old wonder is set to bloom in the next fourteen days for a precious six hours only...'

'Oh, my goodness!' Lavinia literally clutched her pearls, her eyes glittering with girlish excitement as she turned to Joao. 'Joao, you wicked man. You're aware that I must have it, aren't you?' she whispered as a trio of ushers wheeled out a glass pedestal within which a bronze, hand-painted plant pot held a single dark green stem with three, thick purple bulbs branching out at the end. Along the slender stem, several nodes circled the plant, all ready to burst forth with their sacred seed.

Momentarily, Saffie forget her angst as she stared at the rare, exquisite plant. Her research had revealed that the last Shanzi orchid bloomed fifteen years ago. She was in the presence of one of the true wonders of nature.

'What you wish for will be yours. You have my word.'

The words were directed at Lavinia, but when Saffie's gaze lifted, she found Joao staring straight at her.

For a tense few seconds, they traded gazes, and, even though his remained enigmatic, another shiver went through her.

The spell was broken when they were directed to take their seats.

Bidding started at an eye-watering quarter of a million dollars. Joao immediately countered with double the price, and from then encouraged Lavinia to go to town with her bidder's paddle. One by one, the stragglers fell away and he won the bid at three point seven million dollars.

Lavinia clapped with glee as she approached the pedestal to inspect her prize. 'It's simply marvellous.' She turned to Joao and Saffron. 'I'm cancelling all my plans and remaining in Shanghai until this spectacular thing blooms. You two must be there for the event. I insist.'

It was a neat segue for Joao. 'We'll be honoured to join you. And I too must insist you let me treat you to a special dinner to mark the occasion.'

For a hardened businesswoman, Lavinia proved no woman was above Joao Oliviera's charms when she blushed. 'I'd like that.'

'*Sim*. We will leave you to enjoy your gift.'

He caught Saffron's arm and they headed outside to the waiting limo.

Beside her, he lounged but she wasn't deceived by his casual stance. Restlessness prowled his frame, and, in direct effect, escalated her own nerves.

To counteract that, she slid open her tablet. 'I'll organise entertainment for Lavinia while she's in Shanghai and I'll get started on something to mark the blooming—'

'I don't wish to talk about Lavinia. There is such a thing as over-preparation. There comes a time when you need to leave things to play out naturally. Don't you think?'

Saffie frowned. She'd never known Joao not to fine-tune a deal or meeting despite knowing his stuff inside out. But her emotions were still dangerously close to the surface. She risked letting herself down if she didn't borrow a leaf from his book and go with the flow.

She cleared her throat. 'Okay, what would you like to discuss?'

He angled his body towards her, dousing her with that unique scent that made her head spin. When his gaze lingered on the bold red lipstick the stylist had insisted was the only colour to wear with the dress, her blood rushed faster through her veins.

'Your mid-year review is coming up.'

She opened her mouth but he stopped her with a slash of his hand.

'Regardless of whether you intend to leave in three months or not, a review is necessary.'

Apprehension skittered over her. Everything suddenly felt wrong. 'You want to do that now? In the fifteen minutes before we return to the hotel?'

He raised an eyebrow at her. 'You doubt my ability to be efficient?'

'I question your need to do it now, without a member of HR present, as per the company's guidelines.'

He shrugged. 'Call this an informal one, then.'

Before she could object, he carried on. 'One

of your tasks is to take inventory and assess the efficiency of my homes around the world, *sim*?'

'Of course. Did I miss something in my report?' He had twenty-seven residences, all in tip-top shape with a full complement of staff should he be struck with a sudden urge to take a rare vacation.

'According to the latest report, I haven't used my Amalfi Coast property in two years. I've instructed for it to be transferred into your name.'

She went cold, her jaw sagging for several mind-numbing seconds. 'My mid-year bonus is a nine-million-euro *mansion*?'

He scowled at her screechy response. 'No need for hysteria. A simple thank you will suffice. And considering your trying behaviour this week, you can add further thanks for my magnanimity.'

'There's been nothing wrong with my behaviour. I know you said you don't care about appearances but I'd thank you not to scream what happened in Morocco from the rooftops.'

His gaze grew cool. 'I wasn't aware I was doing any such thing.'

'A twenty-bedroom mansion doesn't scream discreet, Joao. It screams *pay-off for services rendered*,' she hissed under her breath, aware of the driver's presence.

Joao hit the partition button, ensuring she was even more alone with him than her excitable senses suggested was wise. 'Don't make it a bigger deal than it is, Saffie. I'm simply rewarding you for your hard work. You will do well to remember that and be grateful.'

'This isn't ingratitude, Joao. This is…way over the top. And if this is in reaction to Will, it's not necessary.'

His tension spiked and she berated herself for mentioning Will. It was clear the other man irritated Joao. Had she done it deliberately, to get a rise out of him?

To what end? To see if he felt something?

'Nevertheless, it is done. My lawyers are in the process of drawing up the papers.'

He said the words with a finality that sent a heavy dose of apprehension skittering over her nerves. 'Joao—'

He wrapped his hands on her upper arms, a dark intimacy trapping them as he brought her flush against his body. 'You're right, it vexes me that Ashby keeps attempting to steal what's mine. But he's not worthy of my attention and you won't go to him because he'll never challenge you the way I do. Now, I'm completely weary of this new argumentative side to you, Saffie. So do me a favour, and stop, hmm?'

Affronted, she opened her mouth to do the opposite. He countered with a simple, devastating act of sealing her mouth with his, stealing her protest and every thought in her head as blazing sensation flared wild and wide through her body.

He made a gruff noise and she realised she'd parted her lips to let him in, her ready invitation crackling the flames higher, straining her body closer to absorb more of the heady sensation.

Where was her circumspection? Her willpower?

Non-existent when it came to him, she was quickly realising.

She needed to get herself under control...and fast.

Because existing in this wild and unfettered state of sensual addiction was dangerous to every single goal she held dear.

CHAPTER FIVE

HE HAD TAKEN clean leave of his senses, allowing that burr of imbalance and dissatisfaction that had taken hold of him recently to inform his actions in a way he hadn't acted since his *favela* days when rash decisions had regularly landed him in trouble.

But this was trouble of the most delicious kind. Trouble he wanted to dive headlong into and feast on, regardless of the consequences.

Sim...the kind that could alter his short- and long-term plans, pave way for his father to get the better of their battle of wills, if he wasn't careful.

He shuddered as Saffie's fingers spiked into his hair, gripping it with a silent demand and breathless enthusiasm that fired his blood and dragged a groan from his throat.

The sound froze them both, their tongues halting that control-shredding dance he yearned to continue. But knew he couldn't.

He needed a little clarity.

Jeopardising this final defining battle with his father was out of the question.

Already he was on edge over his inability to stop thinking about bedding Saffie. That little incident in his study and her calling a halt to it had grated, but uninhibited fumbling in the back of his limo only attested to how badly she affected his control.

With superhuman effort, he eased her away.

Her lips were swollen, beautifully bruised, slick and ripe for another tasting. He hardened painfully, his manhood demanding satisfaction of the most carnal kind with an insistence he hadn't experienced in a long while.

He wanted to have her, to give and receive pleasure, to hear her cry out in that husky voice that set his body aflame.

And the fever of it bewildered him in the extreme.

At his continued perusal, a blush suffused her face. The force with which he wanted to trace that heightened colour with his tongue had him setting her back in her seat.

Meu Deus. Where was the care he'd vowed to take? Where was the reminder that this kind of dangerous blind lust was how *he* himself had come into being? That, like his father, one time hadn't been enough. That Pueblo had given into his baser urges repeatedly until Joao had been created? And then and only then had the man who sired him selfishly slithered away from his responsibilities?

Não, he wouldn't slip down the same path.

For the rest of the journey, he directed his gaze out of the window, stared blindly at the water taxis and boats sailing the Huangpu River as he fought to bring his body back under control.

He exhaled in relief when the driver pulled up to the hotel entrance a few minutes later. He alighted, helped her out and strode quickly for the private lift that serviced his suite.

She didn't speak on their way up.

And he, Joao Oliviera, the man who'd talked himself out of more tricky situations in his precarious youth than he could count, was inarticulate in the grip of unrelenting lust.

He laughed grimly to himself, then even that amusement evaporated when he found he couldn't take his gaze off the racing pulse at her throat. Or her very delectable backside and swaying hips as she exited the lift, the train of her dress caught up in one hand.

Pelo amor de Deus...

He dismissed the hovering butler when they entered the suite, and turned to her, but Saffie got there first.

'This needs to stop,' she announced, her chin raised. 'We have to find a way to be civil without this...*thing* between us.'

He clenched his jaw. 'I agree.'

'You do?'

He should've been pleased at her quickly disguised disappointment. But the need to reverse his own statement almost as soon as he'd uttered it pulled him up short.

He'd fought for her to stay his right hand so he could show Pueblo once and for all that he was more than worthy of the name he'd wished to deprive him off. That he was miles better than any Oliviera. That if he chose to change his name tomorrow, the world would bow to whoever he reinvented himself as.

That if he ever had a child of his own he would—

The alien thought, springing from nowhere, froze him in place.

Doce paraíso!

Why? And why *now* when even abstract thoughts of children had been dismissed with chilling rejection in the past?

Was it Saffie? Had the thought of his assistant flouncing off to create a family at some point in the future crept insidiously into his own subconscious, pushing him to question his own mortality and legacy?

Impossível.

'Joao? Are you all right?'

He throttled back his scowl. 'I don't want any distractions to jeopardise the Archer deal. Lavinia might have been bowled over by the event tonight but we need to capitalise on the advantage, especially in Brazil.'

She dropped the train of her dress, eyes that were more green than blue tonight assessing. 'Because your father will be there?' she probed.

'Because he'll know by morning that I've stepped up the pressure and he will be doing likewise.'

'And you want to win, at all costs?'

The question was soft, curious, unlike any tone she'd used on him before. Absurdly that eroded some of his anger. Not enough, of course, to make him forget that she was sticking her nose where it didn't belong. 'That is none of your business.'

Her chin went up, a taunting little act that made him want to breach the space between them, taste her defiance for himself, then make her yield with soft moans.

'Isn't it? Didn't you all but beg me to stay just

so you could achieve this…whatever vendetta you have against your father?'

'Watch it, Saffie.'

A shadow crossed her eyes and he felt the sting of regret briefly before he stemmed it.

'It may be none of my business but I think you know I care enough about yours to know I won't betray your confidence. Or use anything you tell me in any way other than to help you achieve your goals.'

'Even if you won't approve of them?'

'Would it matter to you?'

Sim, *it would*. The grim realisation disconcerted him, enough for him to jam his hands into his pockets. Beyond the window, Shanghai's spectacular night-time view was a feast for the senses. His gaze skittered over the Bund, Pudong's distinct skyline and the beautifully illuminated outline of City God Temple.

But he wanted a different feast entirely, one that started and ended with gorging on Saffron's body, slaking this hunger overtaking his body and threatening to take over his mind.

His manhood throbbed behind his fly, eagerly offering its consent on the very subject he was fighting. In the window's reflection, he saw her hand rise to her chignon, stroke it nervously. It was a mannerism he realised he'd spotted before but not clocked. What else hadn't he clocked about his assistant?

And why this need to appease her by way of personal divulgences? He had nothing to prove to her.

Conversely, he had nothing to lose by giving her a little insight into his motivations. After all, if it helped her better serve him, where was the harm?

'My father informed me when I was ten that I would amount to nothing.' The words rubbed his throat raw but he smothered the pain. Just as he'd ignored the burrs scraping the wounds of his past. It was baggage he'd had to leave behind lest it dragged him down.

Behind him, Saffie gasped. 'Why would he do that?'

He laughed, a grating sound etched in bitterness he couldn't stem. 'Most likely because of who else helped to sire me? Or perhaps it was because my conception wasn't part of the dirty little tryst he had going on with my mother, if you could even call it that. Except I came along and ruined his perfect life and he decided he'd never fail to remind me where I came from.'

He turned around in time to see her tongue sweep across her lower lip, a distracting action as she grappled with what he'd divulged. 'So he and your mother...had an affair?'

He laughed again. 'An affair? That's a little too civilised a term. My mother was a prostitute, Saffie. They met on a seedy street corner, where she traded her wares near the *favela* where I was born, purely to fuel her drug habit.'

Understanding dawned on her face. 'And your father didn't want to know?'

Bitter tunnelled deeper. 'Of course not. I was the physical manifestation of his recurring weakness. The no-hoper whose geographic circumstances meant I had two choices. Become a drug addict or become a drug dealer.'

'You chose neither option, obviously.'

He started to laugh again but the scar in his palm tingled with a force he hadn't felt since his teenage days. He pulled out his hand and stared down at the jagged white line. The mark that had changed his life. 'No. But it was a very close call.'

'How did you get out of it?'

She'd ventured closer, enough for him to inhale that stimulating scent that seemed programmed to attack his defences.

Voce parece sublime...

She was beyond sublime and he didn't want to further stain her with his past, especially not with secrets he'd guarded with fervent zeal so far. Secrets he would prefer to take to his grave.

'Through the magnanimity of a stranger. That's all you need to know.'

He read the hurt in her eyes and steeled himself against it.

'But your father...what he said...'

He shrugged. 'I decided to prove him wrong. He didn't take the lesson very well. I intend to repeat it until he accepts—'

'You? That's what you want, isn't it? For him to accept you?' she asked softly.

Something fierce tightened in his midriff. Try as he might, Joao couldn't dismiss it.

'Pueblo Oliviera would find that as difficult as swallowing the moon, so no. That's not my aim. But I want him to accept that he will lose every time he pits himself against me. That by the time I'm done we will both know who is the victor.'

A sort of bewildered understanding widened in her eyes, tinged with sadness. Again, he dismissed it.

He didn't need her understanding. Or whatever misplaced sympathy she wanted to bestow on him.

He repeated those words to himself as he approached her. At her nervous glance, he nodded at her necklace. 'Turn around, let me help you with that. Unless you intend to sleep with this on?' Immediately images flashed in his mind of her wearing nothing but the necklace that highlighted her beauty.

When she complied and presented her back to him, it took every control-gathering technique he could summon not to bend his head and trail his lips over her delicate nape. Not to bury his nose in the curve of her neck and inhale deeply, infuse her in his senses.

He completed his task, handed the necklace over and stepped back.

She faced him again, and seemed as if she would push the conversation.

But her eyes widened suddenly, her hand going to her mouth.

He frowned. 'What's wrong?'

Her hand dropped and she shook her head abruptly. 'Nothing. I think something I ate disagreed with me.'

He watched her take a breath, then two. He started to reach for her but she danced out of his way. His jaw clenched. 'Would you like me to summon the doctor?'

'No. I'm fine. It'll pass, I'm sure.' With an abrupt goodnight, she left him standing in the middle of the living room.

Alone, Joao willed his turbulent senses and

heightened libido to settle. But ten minutes of pacing later, he was nowhere near calm.

Work.

That always produced welcome challenges. He could look into Ashby's business, for instance. Embroil the other man in a tussle that would teach him a lesson not to sniff around what didn't belong to him.

He grimaced when not even that spiked an ounce of interest. Everything pressing had been taken care of by Saffie leaving him with a rare freedom he should take advantage of.

But whatever peace he'd hoped for by retreating to his suite, he was woefully denied as night tumbled into dawn.

As he found himself outside Saffie's door, knocking softly before cracking the door open to find her sleeping peacefully.

As he returned to his suite, unable to shake the grim truth from his mind.

Saffie Everhart was well and truly under his skin.

The nausea that had threatened last night in the living room propelled Saffie out of bed moments after she'd opened her eyes. It was strong, immediate and shocking enough to leave her weak and clinging to the porcelain by the time she was done retching.

God…no.

She moaned quietly, unwilling to be overheard despite the vast bathroom that could easily swallow up her whole flat back in Chiswick. She couldn't be ill. Not now when she needed every weapon in her arsenal.

Her night had been disturbed by vivid, lurid dreams of Joao that had left her hot and needy, her sheets twisted with restless yearnings.

She couldn't afford to have her days disrupted by illness, too.

Her temperature wasn't high and her stomach didn't ache. With weak relief, she ruled out food poisoning. She'd sampled a few of Chef Bouillard's delightful concoctions but overall her appetite had been low. Whatever was messing with her system would remedy itself sooner rather than later.

She staggered to her feet, exhaling thankfully when she felt a little better. By the time she'd showered and dressed, only faint shadows remained beneath her eyes to remind her of her restless night and the bathroom mishap.

Her ivory-coloured designer power suit and three-inch heels lifted her spirits and lent much needed confidence as she headed for the dining room.

Joao was sitting at the head of the table, perusing the *Financial Times*. For one stolen second, she froze, their conversation last night unfolding through her mind.

She knew rejection, had felt it deep in her soul each time she'd been passed over at the orphanage. But she couldn't imagine what Joao must've felt when his father had said those horrible, cruel things to him.

It was clear that, like her, he'd used it as fuel to achieve his goals but it was also clear now that it'd left an indelible mark. One he possibly carried inside as well as outside in the form of that scar across his palm. One that made her yearn, impossibly and foolishly, to soothe.

What other damage had it done? Was that why he couldn't accommodate the idea of children? Bewilderingly, her heart lurched at the thought. What did it matter how he felt about children? This journey she intended to take when she was free of him was hers and hers alone.

So why did that idea suddenly further dampen her spirits—?

'Are you going to stand there all morning, Saffie, or would you like to join me so we can start the day?' he drawled in a deep, skin-tingling voice from behind his newspaper.

Saffie jumped, grimacing at the heat that rushed into her cheeks. She approached, momentarily wondering why the superb coffee she usually loved suddenly smelled so strong and pungent, enough to cause her stomach to roil.

Joao lowered his paper and her stomach calmed as if he controlled even *that* somehow.

Dear heaven, he really had no business looking *this* effortlessly magnificent. His Milan-designed grey shirt and matching tie both held a dulled gloss that drew attention to the streamlined torso beneath. Coupled with the hand-stitched pin-striped suit that made his broad shoulders even broader and more powerful, they made Saffie's palms grow clammy with need as Joao's every powerful sensual asset hit her like a sledgehammer.

She grabbed the back of the dining chair for support, the whole effect weakening her knees so she sank into it with less than her customary poise.

If Joao noticed, he chose not to comment. Nevertheless, his gaze scrutinised her face with sizzling thoroughness, and his face clamped into a frown seconds later.

'What's wrong?'

'Excuse me?'

He tossed his newspaper away. 'Are you still unwell?' he asked, angling his mouth-watering body towards her. 'You were sleeping well enough when I checked on you.'

Surprise lit her up. 'You checked on me during the night?'

For the first time in her life, Joao looked anything but supremely arrogant. Even his shrug was a little off. 'Of course. I'm a vampire, you will recall.'

She wasn't fooled by his flippancy. She was more alarmed by the warm softening inside her. The thought that he'd been concerned with her well-being.

Realising he was still scrutinising her face, she hastily answered. 'I'm fine,' she replied, swallowing the disturbing amount of moisture that filled her mouth.

One eyebrow lifted. 'If that's a pat little statement to throw me off the scent, think again. I have eyes, Saffie.'

She reached for her napkin, busied herself with opening it so she wouldn't have to look at him. 'If you ever need another challenge, don't take up the medical profession. Your bedside manner is atrocious.'

'My current position in life satisfies me greatly.

And don't change the subject,' he replied. 'If your stomach still ails you I will call the—'

'I said I'm—' She stopped as the dining-room door opened and the resident tail-coated butler entered, holding aloft a silver platter.

She knew what would be on offer.

Eggs Benedict. Her favourite breakfast. Ordered for her by Joao and prepared by Chef Bouillard.

Saffie felt the ripples in her belly intensify as the butler set the dish down in front of her. Lifted the sterling-silver cloche with a discreet flourish.

'Good morning, ma'am. I hope you will enjoy—'

She lurched away from the table, praying her legs would hold her and her stomach wouldn't disgrace her as she raced for the guest bathroom. She made it just in time to hurl the almost non-existent contents of her stomach. To continue to dry heave as she heard a perfunctory knock before Joao entered.

She squeezed her eyes shut for a few shameful seconds before opening them to glare at Joao, who was pacing the bathroom, his phone glued to his ear, his features grim.

'What are you doing?' she demanded weakly.

'Doing what I should've done last night and summoning the doctor,' he said tensely.

About to tell him not to bother, she was hit with another bout. The hair that had loosened from its knot during her panicked flight from the table unravelled. Before she could reach up, strong hands gathered the tresses, holding them back from her face as her stomach lurched.

Drowning in humiliation, she barely heard Joao hang up. But she felt his fingers brush her temple in soothing strokes as she moaned weakly and attempted to stand.

Strong arms wrapped around her waist and lifted her onto the vanity. She accepted the glass of water he handed her, unable to look at him as she rinsed out her mouth, but when a cool towel dabbed at her forehead, providing merciful relief, she couldn't help but glance into his eyes.

He didn't speak but his gaze was narrowed, teeming with turbulent questions as he administered to her. She chose to face the primary question head-on, her heart suddenly hammering wildly against her ribs.

'It's just a stomach upset.'

His eyebrow spiked again. 'Is it?' he stated coolly.

'What else could it be?'

His lips compressed, and his lashes swept down as he stepped away to run the hand towel under the tap. She watched his fingers curl around the towel, tried hard not to imagine them on her body as he returned to stroke her brow.

'The doctor will provide the answers we need, I'm sure.'

'But I feel fine.'

'Then you won't mind humouring me. Do you feel well enough to move?' he asked, his tone almost gruff.

Frowning at the peculiar throb in his tone, and the building tension in his body, she nodded.

He tossed the towel away. About to hop down, she gasped when he gathered her in his arms, hoisting her high against his chest as he strode out of the bathroom.

'I'm perfectly capable of walking, Joao,' she objected, only for a new weakness to assail her, this time from the warmth of his body and the virile, masculine scent of him, which, unlike the unfortunate breakfast choice, she wanted to inhale in greedy, fervent gulps.

'You're trembling and for the first time since I've known you, you're less than one hundred per cent put together,' he said, his eyes flicking up to her unbound hair, which now trailed over his arm in unfettered waves. 'That tells its own unique story.'

'I'm sorry to disappoint you,' she said a little tartly, then bit her lip.

He laid her down on the large sofa in the living room and flicked open the single button that held her jacket closed. 'It's not an accusation, Saffie.' Again, his voice pulsed with a unique timbre that sent waves of bewildering need to her belly.

Before she could distance herself enough to decipher it, a knock came on the door. The butler answered it and in walked a bespectacled man, introduced as Dr Chang.

Joao rose, shook hands with him before proceeding to take command of the situation.

Quietly astonished, Saffie listened to him list everything she'd eaten and drunk in the past twenty-four hours. Only when the questions got personal did Dr Chang turn to her. 'If you wish privacy, I can—'

She shook her head. 'It's okay, we can speak...' She paused. Somehow, divulging that she and her boss were intimate didn't emerge easily. She cleared her throat. 'But as I told Jo—Mr Oliviera, I'm fine. I'm sure whatever this is will pass soon.'

'Saffie.' His tone was tense, wrapped with that surprising concern again. 'Answer his questions, *por favor*.'

She realised she was fiddling with the hem of her jacket and immediately linked her fingers in her lap.

She concentrated on the doctor's cool touch on her wrist as he took her pulse, counting back to answer the question about her last period.

Quick calculation done, she opened her mouth to relay it, then froze as a bolt of shock went through her.

No, that wasn't right. It couldn't be.

But the deafening clang of her heart dropping like a stone told her it was.

Times and dates that flared like neon signs in her mind.

'Miss Everhart?' the doctor prompted.

Her gaze flew to Joao. He was watching her with brooding, lethal intensity, his body coiled taut as he awaited her answer. 'I... It's been almost nine weeks since I had my period.'

Joao froze completely, his eyes glistening with a stunned light that made her shiver even as a layer of colour receded from his sharp cheekbones.

He jerked forward. 'Nine weeks?' The question was barely a whisper but no less sharp. 'Morocco?'

Her lips tightened. 'Can we talk about this later?'

'This requires a simple yes or no, Saffie.' Again, his voice was hushed. Soft, even. But she wasn't fooled.

She swallowed. '*If* I'm pregnant, then yes.'

His nostrils flared in a long inhalation, his jaw tightening as a cascade of emotions flitted across his face.

'So it is fair to assess that you could be pregnant?' Dr Chang asked.

She swallowed, her senses tumbling into free fall as the ramifications brutally hit home. As the possibility of the fragile and precious life growing inside her drew an awed breath. But how could that be when…? 'I…don't think so… We used protection.'

But even as she said it, something inside her clicked into place, a deep, visceral certainty she couldn't escape.

A fierce joy spiralled through her shock, blooming in her heart even as she felt the centre of her gravity shifting, altering her reality into something that was at once everything she'd ever wanted from the moment she'd understood what family meant, but also something *other* than she'd planned for herself.

Perhaps it was the slow, tectonic change going through Joao that transmitted to her? It was almost imperceptible and he hadn't moved from where he stood but Saffron could feel its immense power, knew that the repercussions of it were yet to fully manifest themselves. But it was coming. Inexorably. Like lava, slow but lethal, flowing down the side of a majestic mountain.

'No contraception is foolproof. Is your cycle regular, Miss Everhart?' Dr Chang asked.

Like clockwork. 'Yes.'

'Then a pregnancy is most likely the answer to your nausea,' he said gently but firmly. 'But a simple test should give you the answers you need.'

She glanced at Joao. He didn't speak but the gleam in his eyes broadcast his thoughts.

Thoughts that matched hers. If she was pregnant…she had to know. 'Do all the tests you need to,' she whispered.

The doctor nodded. 'Of course, miss.'

Joao prowled closer, his gaze skating over her to settle on her belly for one ferocious moment before he refocused on the doctor. 'How long will it take to know for certain?' he demanded in a low, vibrating tone.

'A matter of hours.'

She cleared her throat, drawing the attention of both men. 'Will a blood test tell me how…how far along I am?'

Dr Chang shook his head. 'For that you'll need an ultrasound.'

She glanced at Joao but his gaze was fixed on

the doctor, his body bristling with electric purpose. 'Such a machine is portable, yes?'

Even before he'd opened his mouth Saffie knew the answer was going to be yes. Nothing was beyond the reach of the richest man in the world. 'Yes, the hotel provides a full private medical service to guests.'

Joao's eyes locked on hers, his gaze compelling. 'Is that satisfactory, Saffie?'

Her heart thudded, then expanded to further absorb the news. 'Yes.'

Dr Chang nodded. 'I will make the arrangements.'

'Bom.' Joao gave a satisfied nod without removing his gaze from hers.

Unable to withstand the raw blaze in his eyes, she fixed hers on the doctor. 'Could there be another explanation for the nausea?'

He gave a benign smile. 'Most likely not. According to Mr Oliviera you barely ate anything last night. I'm almost positive this is morning sickness. If you're worried, it goes away after a few weeks. In the meantime, you can combat it with dry crackers and small, frequent meals.'

Joao frowned. 'Crackers?' His suddenly pronounced accent turned even that word sexy.

'They're biscuits, Joao,' she muttered, then forgot that she was using his given name in company. 'I can get them from the shop later.'

'The only place you'll be going is back to bed. Give me the name of the product you need and I'll provide it for you.'

The idea of Joao browsing the shops for crackers almost made her chuckle. But the doctor was opening his bag, readying to take a blood sample. When he was done, he packed up his bag and rose.

Reality hit home harder.

She was pregnant.

A wave of dizziness rushed over her. She swayed in the chair, causing Joao to curse and leap for her. 'Is there something you can give her?' he demanded tersely.

The doctor hesitated. 'I'm reluctant to prescribe anything if she's pregnant. I recommend weak tea, and rest. No matter how strong you are, the news of a child is a little overwhelming.' He gave a small smile. 'I'll be back with definitive news in a few hours.'

Joao walked him out and as she drew a shaky hand over her forehead, Saffie heard them talking in low murmurs. Five minutes later he was back.

'Should I ask what you were talking about?'

Hawk-like eyes watched her as he shrugged

out of his jacket and draped it over a silk-covered chair. 'This is new territory for us. I was merely arming myself with the relevant information.'

'I don't see why. This has nothing to do with you. Besides, I'm aware of what to expect so you don't need to trouble yourself.' She started to rise.

His face, already tightening from her words, stiffened further as he came towards her. 'Sit back down, *por favor*, and explain to me why you think this has nothing to do with me?'

'I can't. Your meeting with the Shanghai team is in forty-five minutes.'

'I cancelled it two minutes ago.'

'Why?'

'Because we have a more pressing situation to deal with, don't you think?'

There it was again, that peculiar note that made alarm tingle at the back of her head.

'You heard the doctor. We… I won't have confirmation for three or four hours. Besides, even if I am, being pregnant isn't a debilitating condition.'

'It is when you barely ate last night and reported that you've thrown up twice this morning. I've instructed the butler to bring you some tea. In the meantime, you will explain what you meant.'

His dark, implacable tone caused a small quake inside her. 'You don't want children, Joao. It doesn't feature in your grand plan, remember. *But I do.*' Her hand crept over her stomach in silent wonder, even while her heart thundered at Joao's continued fierce expression.

He didn't answer for a long minute. 'There's a vast difference between imagination and reality, *querida*,' he breathed softly. 'For instance, I imagined that my own circumstances with my father would be different than they are today. Equally, I imagined that this...*fever* in my blood where you're concerned would have abated by now.'

While she sucked in a stunned breath, he continued. 'But while I'm willing to let go of the one thing, I fully intend to claim the other. Do you understand me?'

She shook her head, almost too afraid to grasp his meaning. 'No. I don't.'

'Let me be clear. I may not have wanted a child but, confronted with the reality of it, you can rest assured that there is no way I will relinquish my claim on my blood.'

As she sat there, grappling with it, he rose, staring down at her with a fierce light gleaming in his eyes she thought would singe her if she looked at him too long. 'We'll discuss this more when you're feeling a little more yourself.'

She wanted to laugh, but sudden rising hysteria advised her to curb the urge. If she was truly pregnant—and the subtle changes in her body she'd put down to her agitated state suddenly pointed to that status—then her life was changed for ever.

Dr Chang returned just before midday.

Saffie, having managed to keep down a piece of dry toast and two cups of tea, stood in the middle of the living room. Aware of Joao's imposing presence beside her, she linked her fingers in front of her as Dr Chang entered. The two technicians who followed, wheeling in a large ultrasound machine, couldn't have spelled out her condition louder if it'd been written in fifty-foot letters in the sky.

The room spun around her but Saffie wasn't aware she'd moved until Joao's arm wrapped firmly around her waist.

'This is our new reality, Saffie,' he rasped softly, almost soothingly, in her ear. His voice was gruff, but there was a layer of intent as he watched her that drew goosebumps across her flesh.

Dr Chang approached, leaving the butler and

technicians at a discreet distance as he gave a shallow bow. 'Miss Everhart, I have the results of your blood test.' He cast a quick look behind him. 'You can probably guess what it is. Congratulations.'

Her nod was shaky, her heart hammering against her ribs so hard she feared she would pass out. 'Thank you,' she murmured.

'Would you still like me to perform the ultrasound?'

Beside her Joao stiffened, a coiled tension seizing his frame.

'Yes, thanks.'

Joao relaxed a touch, his arm temporarily drifting over her hip before claiming her waist once more.

Within minutes, she was lying on her bed, Joao's overwhelming presence beside her as Dr Chang rolled the wand over the cold gel on her abdomen.

When the coloured 3D image appeared on the screen, Saffie's heart leapt into her throat. A moment later, a rapid heartbeat joined the picture. A breath of wonder shuddered out of her, her eyes prickling as she watched the wriggling bean on the screen.

Her baby. Her family. Every hope and aspiration within reach. But as she watched the dancing blob, Saffie's breath caught for another reason. For as long as she'd yearned for this dream, she'd pictured just herself and her baby. Two against the world.

In all the years of hoping and dreaming, all she'd wanted was a mother. Someone to hold her close, tell her she mattered. Perhaps because she knew it was her mother who'd left her behind, she'd been the parental figure Saffie had wanted the most. A father had been an even more impossible dream. One totally out of her reach.

But now she was faced with an even more impossible scenario.

The shadowy shape of the stranger who would one day father her child had now taken the form of the most formidable man she'd ever met. The richest man in the world, with endless power and influence, who would remain way out of her league for ever. A man who intended to claim her baby, but not her.

That bruising reminder that all she was good for was the Archer deal made her heart lurch, clouding her joy.

Dr Chang made a sound under his breath, his brow furrowing slightly as he stared at the screen.

'What is it?' Joao demanded fiercely.

'Well, first of all I can confirm that you're indeed approximately nine weeks pregnant.' He moved the wand a short distance, paused, and then smiled. 'And I can also confirm that there isn't just one foetus but two.'

Joao's nostrils pinched as he inhaled sharply. *'O que voce disse?'*

'What?' They both demanded at the same time.

'Miss Everhart is carrying twins,' the doctor said, his even voice confirming the thunderbolt he'd just delivered.

Fresh shock powered through Saffie, her hand flying to her mouth. 'Oh, my God!'

'It's too early to determine the sex but you can do that in a few weeks if you wish.'

She made the mistake—or perhaps it was a fortunate occurrence—of looking at Joao then as his gaze moved from the screen to her stomach. And stayed.

There is no way I will relinquish my claim on my blood.

Her heart hammered.

If his words hadn't driven his intention home before, it certainly did now.

'Joao…'

'Not now, Saffie.' His lashes swept down as if shielding his thoughts from her. She wanted to believe he was shaken by the news but she couldn't be certain. Not with that fierce light she'd glimpsed in his eyes.

After the machine was wheeled out, Dr Chang delivered a short lecture on pre-natal care, left her with the appropriate vitamins, then made himself scarce.

Joao, who'd planted himself at the window of her bedroom, finally turned around when they were alone.

For the longest moment he said nothing.

Nerves ate at her as she slid out of bed. 'We need to talk.'

'Were you on the Pill in Morocco?'

She inhaled sharply, sagging back into bed. 'I hope you're not suggesting this was a deliberate act on my part?'

He frowned. 'That did not occur to me. I'm merely trying to work out the evolution of our current situation.'

Our situation. Two words that drove home in no uncertain terms that he'd placed himself firmly in the middle of her future. 'Oh, Okay. Well, thank you. No, my old Pill wasn't agreeing with me so I was between prescriptions. I didn't say anything that night because you used protection when we...'

His eyes glinted darkly. 'When we had sex. It's not a dirty word, Saffie.'

She flushed. 'I know it's not.'

'Protection which failed, obviously.'

Her breath shuddered out and she couldn't stop her hand from stealing over her stomach.

Twins. Conceived on the night when she'd gone insane and thrown caution to the wind. A night that was about to come back to haunt her?

She flicked a glance at Joao's face but, with the sunlight at his back, his expression was unreadable.

'Obviously this changes things,' he intoned.

A vice tightened around her chest, making her light-headed. 'In what way?'

He sent her a droll, mocking look. 'In every way you can think of, I imagine.' He strolled towards the door. 'But at your insistence, I rescheduled my meeting with the Shanghai team, so we'll have to dig further into this later.'

She rose, straightening her clothes as she followed him out. 'I'll tell the driver to meet us downstairs in five minutes.'

He stopped with a hand on the front door. 'I'm going alone, Saffie.'

The vice around her chest tightened. 'Why? Have I suddenly turned invalid?'

'No, you haven't. But you *are* carrying twins. And whether you wish to admit it or not, news like that takes getting used to. I'm simply giving you the time to accustom yourself to it. And I would prefer it if you did that in bed.'

'So why does that sound uncannily like an order?'

He released the door and retraced his steps back to her. Without warning he spiked his fingers into her loosely bound hair, and one thumb grazed over her lower lip. 'I don't doubt your ability to shoulder this news and do your job. But I think you need time to absorb the news properly, do you not?'

Her chin lifted. 'Are you calling me emotional, Joao?'

'*Sim*, I am,' he stated boldly.

And to her eternal shame, she confirmed it with a great big lip wobble, one overwhelming feeling after another chasing through her.

He caressed her again with his thumb, before he stepped back and started to walk away.

'"I need you." "I want you to stay." "I'll do anything to achieve that." Any of those words ring a bell, Joao?'

He froze, then whipped around to face her. 'No. I haven't forgotten.' His gaze dropped to her stomach, an inferno of possessiveness in his eyes. 'But I also protect what's mine, Saffron.'

Before she could find adequate words to counter that, he was gone. And traitorously her weakened legs necessitated her do exactly as he'd said.

She crawled back into bed.

Joao realised his hands were shaking as he sat back in the leather seat of his limo, exhaling as it pulled away from beneath the hotel's portico.

Deus, his whole body was shaking.

Twins.

His first absurd thought when the doctor had delivered the news was that he'd willed them into existence with thoughts of heirs and legacies last night.

His second was...*why twins?*

But then the searing reminder that he had no real clue as to his family tree hit home. Everything he'd bothered to find out about Pueblo Oliviera revolved around the man's business interests, with a brief investigation into any possible adverse genetic traits he might have inherited. He had dozens of files on the former and just enough to satisfy himself on the latter.

But what moved him next, what continued to prowl relentlessly through him now, was the complete and utter *need* to claim what was rightfully his. The need to protect the investment he hadn't even known he was making when he'd succumbed to his desires that night in Morocco.

He grimly admitted to himself that he'd left Saffie behind partly because *he* needed time to come to terms with the emotions rampaging through him. And, yes, to strategise in light of this new development.

She was bearing his child. His children. His... *heirs*.

A cold wave of shock was followed by the hot grip of determination.

No way was she leaving him now.

For a man who'd never thought in such terms, the realisation was profound and bracing enough to drive his fingers through his hair.

But, adversely, accepting his new reality wasn't as testing as he'd imagined. Perhaps it was even divine intervention, giving him another chance to best his father.

Sim.

He relaxed against the seat as his limo whisked him into the financial heart of Shanghai, acknowledging the savage intent twining with a peculiar elation swelling inside him.

He hadn't planned for this, but, as he'd said to Saffie, reality brought its own specifications.

And this demanded complete and utter lock down of both his children and the woman who carried them.

He would stamp his legacy on his heirs, make the worthless Oliviera name mean something.

Finally.

CHAPTER SIX

SAFFIE ROSE AN hour later, dressed and summoned her car.

She didn't need to consult her electronic diary to know Joao's next meeting would be starting in twenty-five minutes.

Blessed with light traffic, she arrived just as his staff were taking their seats around the large conference table.

Joao's eyes widened, then narrowed fiercely on her face as she took up her position next to him and fired up her tablet.

'Saffie,' he breathed. 'What are you doing here?'

'My job, Joao. And, yes, before you ask, my power nap did wonders for me. Your people are waiting. Would you like to start?'

His jaw clenched but while his thunderous gaze suggested he was considering throwing everyone out, after a charged minute he swivelled his chair away and addressed his COO.

The meeting finished two hours later. Knowing he was going straight into another video-conference and would be tied up for most of the afternoon, she typed up the meeting notes, then caught up her bag.

Outside, she dismissed her driver, hoping that a walk would provide enlightenment about what carrying Joao's babies meant now he'd vowed to claim them.

She crossed over from Pudong to Old City Shanghai, trailed her way through the stunning temples in Yu Garden and arrived at her destination with one clear thought.

She wouldn't give up her desire to form a unit with her babies. Not for Joao. Or anyone.

The members-only Xinqu Tea House was situated in a tastefully converted temple, complete with stunning Chinese screens and miniature tinkling waterfall over smooth stones.

Every aspect of the tea house was designed to soothe the senses.

Joao's arrival barely five minutes after her exquisite tea was served put paid to her desire for calm.

The sight of him striding towards her minus his tie, with the top buttons of his shirt undone, sparked naked flames of lust through her.

Without invitation, he seated himself across from her, his eyes pinning her in place.

'You left without telling me. Or telling your driver where you were going.'

'Which begs the question, how did you find me?'

His jaw rippled. 'What exactly are you trying to prove, Saffie?'

'I just wanted to clear my head. And have some tea.'

'Clear your head of what?'

She pressed her lips together. She couldn't tell him what she hadn't worked out for herself. And even if she did, what were the chances he would accommodate her wish to keep her children? Exclusively?

'Saffie?' His voice throbbed with warning. 'I hope the fact that your current circumstance doesn't strictly fall in with your original plans doesn't mean you intend to do anything foolish.'

She frowned. 'Foolish? Like what?'

His eyes darkened and he pursed his lips as if he didn't want to voice the words.

Several seconds ticked by before Saffie grasped his meaning. She gasped, her hand flying to her stomach. 'You think... I would never!'

Tension eased out of him. The fisted hand on the table loosened. *'Bom.'* The single word throbbed with feeling. 'As long as we're on the same page.'

But her senses were flailing at the very thought of even considering what he'd thinly accused her of.

'Of course we are. This is all I've...' She stopped and took a breath. 'I intend to cherish my children, Joao. Make no mistake about that,' she vowed with a voice that trembled with the depth of her emotion.

Something shifted in his eyes and he stared at her long and hard before he nodded. 'Your point is well made, Saffie. As is the other point you made in my boardroom.'

'Good, then I too am glad we're on the same page.'

They weren't. Not completely. She didn't know exactly what he intended to do with regard to the babies she carried.

But Saffie had had enough emotional shocks for one day.

Tomorrow was soon enough to slay the next dragon.

The knock came on the door just after seven the next morning.

Saffie, attempting to remain completely still in a bid to quiet her roiling stomach, called out a weak, 'Come in,' expecting the butler or another member of the suite staff.

Joao strode in with a large sterling-silver tray in hand.

She gasped, sat up a little too hurriedly and triggered a strong protest in her stomach. Her fingers flew to her mouth, and she sent a fervent prayer to not disgrace herself.

Halfway across the floor, he froze. 'Are you all right?'

She took several deep breaths. 'Sudden movements aren't conducive to holding morning sickness at bay, I'm finding.'

He nodded. 'I'm told it's to be expected.'

She eyed him as he strolled forward, brimming with mouth-watering vitality while she felt like several paler versions of herself. 'What are you doing here?' she asked when he simply looked down at her.

He deposited the tray across her lap. 'It's recommended that you have something to eat before you get out of bed, is it not?'

Glancing down, she saw the tray contained a pot of tea, a few condiments and a brand of crackers she'd only ever seen in one place. 'These crackers are sold exclusively at Winthrop's in New York.' She knew because she'd purchased them as part of Oliviera's senior executives' Christmas hamper last year.

'*Sim*, they are. I contacted your assistants and

they informed me these were the best. I had them flown in overnight.'

Her mouth dropped open. 'You had a box of crackers flown in?'

'Several boxes to see you through this phase of your pregnancy. You need them to combat your condition. It's no big deal, Saffie.'

Not to him, obviously. The richest man in the world only needed to click his fingers for his every whim to be fulfilled.

And you're carrying his children.

If she was honest with herself, that hooded, claiming look in his eyes had kept her tossing and turning last night. Because if there was one thing she knew well, it was how relentless Joao could be when he pursued a business deal.

And this was way more than a business deal.

She'd given herself a night's grace. She couldn't afford to bury her head in the sand any longer.

Her hand moved towards the teapot as she contemplated how to tackle the subject. But it froze when she realised Joao was staring at her. Specifically, at her hair.

'Something wrong?' she asked a little tartly because she knew she didn't look her best.

His gaze stayed on her hair for another second before meeting hers. 'I've never seen you with your hair down,' he said, a low throb in his voice.

Her fingers flew up, self-consciously curling around a long strand of hair. 'Oh.'

The atmosphere thickened, enveloping them in a heavy, sensual bubble as he freed the strand and wrapped it around his own fingers. *'E lindo,'* he murmured.

She knew what that meant. *Beautiful.*

Against the brush of her satin and lace nightie, her breasts, suddenly ultra-sensitive, grew heavy, their peaks hardening in reaction to his voice, his scent, his caress.

Joao's gaze dropped to the visible signs of her arousal, his Adam's apple moving in a thick swallow as he deepened the caress, his fingers gently threading through her hair in a hypnotic caress.

The tray in her lap forgotten, Saffie leaned into his touch, cravings heightened and firing between her thighs. But when a moan surged up her throat, she realised what she was doing, how easily she was falling under his spell.

She pulled herself back, one hand dragging up the sheet to cover her chest.

His gaze remained on the tendril caught between his fingers. Then he tucked it behind her ear and met her gaze. The fiery hunger in his eyes nearly undid her. She grasped the handle of the delicate teapot a little desperately, and concentrated on pouring a cup.

When he hitched one thigh up and sat down on the side of the bed, Saffie struggled not to be affected by his potent proximity.

She took a sip of tea and scrambled to think beyond her all-consuming arousal. 'Did everything go smoothly with the Macau team? You hadn't returned by the time I went to bed.' They'd returned to the office after their stop at the tea house but she'd left him to return to the hotel after setting up his last meeting.

One eyebrow spiked. 'Were you waiting up for me, Saffie?'

She felt a blush creep up her neck. She'd waited up for him until sudden weariness had descended on her at an unconscionable nine p.m. 'Only because we needed to talk.'

His face hardened slightly. '*Sim*, we do. But perhaps not yet.'

Her pulse tripped. 'What do you mean?'

His response was to pick up the small platter of crackers and hold it out to her. 'Eat,' he urged firmly.

She took one tiny bite into the dry but exquisite wheat cracker and washed it down with another sip of tea. Realising he wasn't going to engage in their discussion until she'd eaten, Saffie ate a few more, relieved when her stomach showed no signs of rebelling against the meal.

With a decisive click, she set the cup down and cleared her throat. 'I've eaten. Let's talk.'

His gaze moved slowly over her face, lingering on her tingling mouth for several seconds before he abruptly rose and padded over to the window. She couldn't help but follow the pure animal grace of his movement.

'Now that one of your primary reasons for wanting to leave me is…taken care of, is it fair to say that you'll be staying?' he asked without turning around.

She frowned. She wanted to say yes, but the vivid warning that she was wandering further into dangerous territory emotionally stayed her tongue. But wasn't it already too late? By falling pregnant with his children, hadn't she ensured a permanent link with him? 'I… I don't know.'

He swivelled on his heel, his gaze hooded. 'When will you know?'

'Why?'

'Because my next decision depends on it.'

'What decision?'

His lips pressed flat in a formidable line. 'Nothing that cannot wait until we've dealt with Lavinia. But going forward, you should know I've instructed HR to hire two more assistants for you. And from now on, there'll be a personal doctor with us when we travel.'

Her frown intensified. 'Are you trying to make me feel like some…exotic animal on exhibit in a zoo?'

'*Que?* What are you talking about?'

'Hiring more assistants? What is that if not sending a message that I'm either overworked or something else is up with me? And a doctor? Why don't you shine a spotlight on me while you're at it? Announce to the world that your executive assistant is pregnant and you happen to be the father!'

His jaw clenched. 'Saffie—'

'No. I want this to be a normal pregnancy—'

'Well, it is not!'

The quiet thunder of his response froze her into stillness, her vocal cords ceasing to work as she watched him prowl back to her bedside.

'Once the customary twelve weeks have passed, we will revisit the subject of whether you're staying or leaving. I trust you'll have arrived at a decision by then?'

She opened her mouth to argue, then closed it again. She knew the statistics, knew that the first trimester was the most precarious, with the risks higher with multiple babies. Her hand smoothed over her belly, her heart squeezing at the thought of the worst happening. It wouldn't.

It just...*couldn't.*

As for the Archer deal, they'd worked hard for it and she wanted to see him win it. She ignored the *why* that pulsed hard and insistent at the back of her mind. Smothered the voice suggesting that, after his revelations about his father, her emotions were entangled with the deal that should've been purely professional. 'Yes,' she answered him.

Satisfaction lit his eyes. 'Good. Join me when you're ready. I've put together a counter-proposal for the takeover of that Qatar company Pueblo was dealing with.'

She didn't remind him that it was Sunday.

In fact, Saffie was secretly thrilled that, while this new part of her life seemed poised on some unknown precipice, her work life was mostly stable.

She joined him in the suite's study thirty minutes later, and, besides the heated scrutiny he gave her form-fitting lilac dress, Joao easily slotted into billionaire magnate mode.

It set the tone for the next week.

And when Lavinia announced that her prized orchid looked set to bloom within forty-eight hours, Saffie sent out the invitations for Lavinia's party.

After the stops she'd pulled out to ensure an unforgettable event at short notice, it was satisfying to see the RSVPs flood in almost immediately, the event bold and unique enough to become the talk of the business world within hours.

Even Joao cracked a smile when he saw her plans.

'You've outdone yourself, Saffie,' he drawled, then leaned forward to trace her cheek with his fingers. 'I knew you wouldn't let me down.'

The words burrowed deep, wrapping warmly around her heart in a way she knew was unwise but she couldn't have stopped if her life depended on it. To combat the sensation, she replied briskly, 'Don't thank me just yet. It's costing you an eye-watering bundle.' Seven million dollars, to be precise, a sum that still made her feel a little sick when she thought of it. But then he'd given her a twenty-million slush fund to play with and since Lavinia had kept to her word and stayed in Shanghai, impressing her felt essential.

Joao shrugged. 'The return will be worth it, I'm confident.'

His deep confidence in her abilities further

lightened her heart until Saffie felt as if she were floating on a cloud of happiness.

By Sunday evening, though, nerves were eating at her. She stood in front of a long gilt-edged mirror in her dressing room, her gaze flitting over her cream floor-length gown.

Even though she knew it was too early to be showing, the dress that had felt comfortable just a week and a half ago suddenly felt a little too snug at the bust and waist, the hint of cleavage suddenly too…ripe.

The asymmetrical bodice was studded with multi-hued Swarovski crystals, their brilliance throwing into relief skin turned a light golden from the sun and the luxury cosmetics she'd pampered herself with during her hour-long bath. She bit her lip, unsure about leaving her hair down.

The hairdresser that came with stylist team exclusively serving the suite had gushed about her hair, exclaimed it was a sin to keep it bound and so had styled it into thick, wavy curls over one shoulder, lending her an elegant look.

Thankfully, tonight her jewellery was a little more modest. The heart-shaped diamond hanging from its white platinum chain didn't compete with the crystals in her gown.

With a decisive nod she swivelled from the mirror.

Traversing long marble-floored corridors lined with stunning, priceless works of art, she stepped into the living room and found Joao at the window, his gaze on the view.

Excitement kicked into her throat when he swivelled to face her. The hand lifting the crystal tumbler of cognac to his lips froze halfway, his body stilling as he stared at her.

He muttered something she didn't understand.

She made a moue of annoyance, even while her skin tingled giddily at his intense scrutiny. 'If that's a compliment, I really wish you would say it in English so I understand. Unless I'm mistaken and you're making a joke at my expense?'

The barest hint of a smile accompanied the quirk of his brow. Both expressions fizzled away as he approached, every step rendering her breathless. 'It's a compliment but one that loses its power in translation so you'll just have to step up your efforts to learn my language.'

Saffie chose not to tell him that she'd begun listening to Portuguese language tapes in bed at night, both for that purpose and because over the last week it'd dawned on her that her children would be half Brazilian. And going on the promise she'd made to herself, she wouldn't fail them in any aspect of their heritage, the way she'd been failed.

She plastered on a cool smile. 'In that case, thanks.'

'De nada.' His gaze roved over her, lingering on her hair.

Bracing herself for another comment, she watched his lids sweep down to veil his expression before he tossed back his drink.

'Shall we?'

She nodded. 'Guess so.'

He eyed her. 'You don't sound very confident, Saffie.'

'It was a feat to pull this off. I'm just worried about last-minute glitches.'

He flicked a hand in arrogant dismissal. 'There won't be any. I won't permit it.'

She almost laughed. But then he held out his arm to her in a smooth, gallant gesture that caused her throat to dry up.

Her fingers slid over his tuxedoed forearm, her heart flipping over as she encountered his tensile strength. It took a study in composure not to stumble over her own feet as they walked to the lift.

Downstairs, he helped her into the plush seat of the Rolls, buckled her in before seeing to his own.

The evening was clear, the temperate weather

set to hold for the duration of the party. But nerves continued to attack her for the twenty-five-minute drive to the Lupu Bridge.

Right up until Saffie witnessed for herself the fruits of her labour.

She knew her request for the bridge to be shut for a private event hosted by the richest man in the world had been granted in theory. But seeing it first-hand, with electric-blue spotlights illuminating the bridge, the red carpet stretching from one end of the visually stunning bridge to the other, and ten same-colour-themed tables elaborately decorated for their guests, made her heart swell, her sense of accomplishment extremely satisfying.

They alighted and were escorted by white-gloved liveried footmen to the sound of a string quartet serenading guests as they mingled and enjoyed cocktails.

As a pre-birthday event for the woman whose business Joao intended to acquire, it was second to none, and when the guest of honour arrived, Saffie held her breath as Lavinia alighted from her limo.

The look on her face as she stared up at the thousands of lights strung up around the single, wide arc of the bridge was awestruck.

'I told you that you had nothing to worry about,' Joao drawled from beside her.

She turned to him, and the effect of the devastatingly stunning smile he sent her hit her squarely in the solar plexus. She was still recovering from it as he walked her down the long red carpet to the middle of the bridge and the centre table laid out with pristine silverware and a breathtaking centrepiece flower arrangement, and candelabras that had cost ten thousand dollars each.

Lavinia beamed, holding out both hands to Joao as she reached the table.

'I didn't think you could outdo yourself, Joao, but you've proved me wrong.'

'You're not the first to underestimate my determination, Lavinia. Or my considerable skills.' The words were warm but the undertone of steel was unmissable.

Several guests at the table, mostly Lavinia's executives and family, greeted Joao with reverence as he held out Saffie's chair, then folded his impressive frame into the seat between hers and Lavinia's.

'But again, the person who is responsible for all this is Saffron.'

Lavinia's gaze flicked to her, and she blinked.

'I'm beginning to see she's a priceless asset. Take care you don't lose her.'

Whisky-gold eyes caught and locked on hers. 'I have no intention of doing so.'

Saffie's heart flipped again, and, even though she told herself it was foolish, her emotions chose to remain feverishly buoyant all through the pre-dinner cocktails and canapés service. And if anyone noticed she was drinking sparkling water instead of vintage Dom Perignon, they chose not to comment on it.

Conversation flowed, many guests including high-ranking political figures, heirs and heiresses, and A-list stars approaching to schmooze Joao while attempting to bask in his unique limelight. Saffie watched him mingle, exuding effortless charm, and she wondered how a boy who'd grown up in the slums of Brazil had risen to this. What had he sacrificed? Did that sacrifice still weigh on him?

She was pondering that when he stopped mid-conversation with another guest and speared her with fierce eyes. 'Something wrong?'

Saffie blushed, a little embarrassed at being caught gawking. 'No, nothing at all.'

He continued to watch her for another long spell, then, without warning, wrapped his hand around her waist, pulled her close and carried on with his conversation.

Saffie was too stunned to react so she stayed put, and when the head waiter came and whispered in her ear that the next segment of the evening was ready, she berated herself for the hollow that assailed her when she moved from Joao's side.

The six-course dinner went off without a hitch, with each course drawing stunned murmurs from the guests.

But the pièce de résistance came during the dessert course, when a spotlight at the highest point of the bridge's arch illuminated a single figure dressed in a white three-piece suit. Guests hushed as the first sweet strains from a violin filled the air. For a breathtaking minute, the violinist played from a stationary position, then was slowly lowered by a tensile cable.

The sound swelled, beautiful and enchanting, until he landed smoothly on his feet beside Lavinia, then knelt on one knee to finish off the exquisite piece.

Then, while the last echoes of the violin faded, the excited usher tasked with caring for the Shanzi orchid approached.

With one hundred honoured guests gathered around the pedestal that held the rare plant, they watched the first bud slowly part to reveal the black, cream and purple striped orchid. For a soul-stirring fifteen minutes each bud flowered, gifting them with its beauty and sweet scent.

As the last bud burst open, thunderous applause echoed on the bridge.

Lavinia dabbed discreetly at her eyes as she went to the pedestal and picked up the newly flowered plant. 'My goodness, now the plans I have for my own birthday celebrations look mediocre compared to this.'

'Hopefully you'll have a great reason to make it special,' Joao said as he escorted her back to their table.

'Perhaps I will,' she said cryptically.

An hour later, when Joao leaned close to Saffie and murmured, 'You pulled it off. Bravo,' she couldn't help the relieved smile that broke over her face.

His breath audibly caught.

'Something wrong?' she asked, her own voice trembling.

His molten gaze raked her face. Then, 'Everyone is singing your praises. I think I need to redouble my efforts to ensure you stay.'

Saffie opened her mouth but whatever answer her brain was scrambling to come up with was halted when Lavinia cleared her throat delicately.

'I had lunch with your father a few days ago.'

Joao stiffened, an arctic chill sweeping over his features. 'Did you?' he replied silkily.

Lavinia gave an enigmatic smile. 'Hmm. I heard his vision for my company. It's interesting to say the least.'

He smiled grimly. 'By interesting you mean you know he intends to break up your company in little pieces and sell every last scrap for profit even while assuring you it's the best solution for your legacy?'

A wave of sadness passed over Lavinia's face. 'He wasn't as plain-speaking as that.'

'No. I bet he wasn't. But in case you're doubting your instincts, that's exactly what he'll do given the chance.'

She sipped her champagne before setting the glass down. 'It's difficult to imagine one's life work headed for the scrapheap.'

'Then why are you resisting me?' he enquired smoothly.

She toyed with the stem of her wine glass, her shrewd eyes meeting Joao's. 'Because I'm not completely convinced you're not your father's son.'

Saffie felt the silent fury vibrating off Joao. But Lavinia put her hand over his. 'I'm sorry if that sounds harsh but you wanted to know my reservations? There they are.'

After nerve-shredding silence, Joao nodded. 'I appreciate that. Perhaps you'll give me a chance to prove you wrong.'

Lavinia sat back, her eyes gleaming at the prospect of another adventure. 'How on earth can you top this?' She indicated the spectacular setting.

'Easily. Come to Brazil.'

'I've already been. Many times.'

His smile was steeped in self-assurance. '*Sim*, but not *my* Brazil.'

She lifted her glass and took another long sip. 'After what you've shown me tonight, I'm excited to see what else you have up your sleeve.'

Joao nodded before his gaze hardened. 'I do, however, have one condition. Before you leave Brazil you will give me an answer. I'm a busy man with other interests to pursue.' His eyes flicked to Saffie and she felt her insides dip. 'Interests I do not wish to put off much longer. Are we agreed?' His gaze remained on her for several seconds before returning to spear Lavinia's.

The older woman's gaze shifted to Saffie and without a doubt Saffie knew she was reading between lines and coming up with her own conclusions.

'We're agreed. And now I must leave. Sadly, as much as I wish otherwise, I need a minimum of eight hours' sleep to function.' She rose and held her hand out to Joao, who took it and brushed a gallant kiss across the back of it.

The last of the guests departed shortly thereafter, leaving behind a charged, electric silence. The quartet still played softly in the background, and the look in the eyes that rested on her made every cell in her body tingle.

'Joao—'

'Dance with me,' he demanded abruptly.

'I… What?'

He pushed his chair back, rose and held out his hand. 'We have this place to ourselves till midnight. It'll be a shame to let it go to waste, no?'

Saffie swallowed the lump in her throat. The force of the need driving through her made her limbs weak, her heart hammer with giddy exhilaration at the thought of being held within those strong arms, enveloped in that stunning magnificence that was Joao Oliviera.

'I'm waiting, Saffie,' he murmured, supremely seductive.

She took a breath. And gave into the weakness.

It was for one magical night, a moment in time.

She slid her hand into his, let him tug her up, draw her to his powerful body.

One large hand splayed on her back, the other catching her hand in his and laying their entwined fingers against his broad shoulder.

As if conjured up by the same magic swirling around them, the violinist reappeared and started a slow, seductive tune, one that required only a simple swaying of bodies across red-carpeted asphalt.

The enthralling scent of him.

The seductive warmth of his body.

The intoxicating power he exuded so effortlessly.

The combination was almost too much to bear.

So when, after they'd swayed in a full circle, his lips brushed over her temples, Saffie closed her eyes, sighed, and surrendered to the hypnosis. And when he gathered her closer, until her breasts tingled and her nipples peaked against his chest, all she could do was give a low moan and tuck her face into the crook of his shoulder, and dream for a moment that she belonged.

That she wasn't alone in the world with only the promise of the babies growing inside her to give her hope.

She wasn't sure how long they danced, only that she never wanted the moment to end. Never wanted to face the reality that included admitting that she was experiencing more than a surge of pregnancy hormones. That she was straying, or probably had already strayed, into the dangerous territory of unprofessional, unacceptable feelings for Joao Oliviera.

Her boss.

A warning tingle of self-preservation attempted to rise.

Another brush of Joao's mouth down the side of her neck dissolved it.

'I want you, Saffie.' The statement was raw, pulsing with savage hunger that drew a decadent shudder through her and drained every last ounce of resistance she'd thought to summon. 'Just for tonight, I want you to be mine.'

One night only.

Dared she do it?

Yes, came her heart's fierce response.

Still she hesitated, waiting for a sign that never came, while the desperate clamouring in her heart built and built, until she could do nothing but raise her head, meet his heated gaze full on.

'Then have me,' she said simply.

His eyes turned almost black, only a tiny dark gold around his iris blazing down at her.

Without speaking he gripped her hand in his and walked her down the carpet to where the Rolls waited. The driver, spotting them approach, opened and held the back door.

Saffie got in, followed quickly by Joao, and between one breath and the next the lilting strains of the violin were cut off and nothing but their urgent breathing filled the private enclosed space.

They leapt towards each other at the same time, rabid hunger dictating their movements. Joao spiked his fingers into her hair to angle her face for the hard pressure of his mouth.

She moaned as his tongue breached her lips to boldly taste her. She strained into his touch, eager for every kiss and caress now that she'd permitted herself to take this night for herself.

Joao delivered, savouring her like fine wine. And like fine wine he went straight to her veins, rousing her senses to life.

The partition was up so when he captured her waist and repositioned her in his lap, brushing away the folds of her gown until her centre was boldly imprinted on his groin, she didn't hold back her moan.

With one hand, he tugged her away from the kiss, then with deliberate, wicked movement, he dragged her hips over his engorged length.

'Oh, God,' she gasped as fire blazed through her bloodstream.

He smiled, a wicked and thrilling smile that made her heart lurch, then thunder wildly. She fell into another kiss, welcoming the hand that cupped her breast.

They stayed like that for the short drive back, and she was thankful when Joao gruffly instructed his driver to deliver them to the VIP entrance.

Within minutes they were stumbling into the living room. He swept her off her feet and strode confidently into the master suite.

Her dress came off in seconds and Saffie stood naked before Joao.

He took his time looking at her as he disrobed. 'This is the first time I've seen you truly naked.'

For some reason that struck a vein of apprehension in her heart. She dammed the feeling, telling herself she had nothing to fear.

This was only for tonight.

'And?' she asked, a whisper of cheekiness striking her.

'And you're even more beautiful than I imagined you to be,' he returned thickly.

She swayed beneath the power of his words. He caught her easily, laying her out on the bed, and finished undressing.

Then his hard, beautiful body was covering hers, his mouth tasting every inch of skin he located until he reached her breasts, and slowed his pace.

He moulded the heavy globes, blew a wicked little breeze across the stiff peaks and sent several shudders racing through her.

'Too sensitive?'

Blushing, she nodded.

Lowering his head, he kissed around the areola for endless minutes, before, his eyes tracking her every involuntary reaction, he sucked her flesh into his mouth.

'Joao,' she groaned, clutching the back of his head as sensation pummelled her.

'You were beautifully responsive before, but now you're simply...breathtaking.'

Another helpless moan left her lips as his expert fingers slid between her legs, caressed her, then mercilessly teased the sensitive nub at the apex of her thighs.

She cried out, her fingers clutching blindly at him. 'I need... I need...'

'Tell me what you need, *querida*, and it will be yours,' he commanded.

'I need you...inside me. Please.'

His nostrils flared and she felt a fine tremor shake his body before he levered himself over her. Fingers sliding into her hair, Joao angled his lean hips between her thighs. His gaze fused to hers, he entered her with one powerful thrust and settled himself deep inside her.

He fell on the moan that ejected from her throat, devouring it as if it belonged to him. Then he angled her head up.

'Look at me, Saffie.'

She dragged half-closed eyes open, met his fiery ones.

'Wrap your legs tighter around me,' he ordered gruffly.

When she did, he shuddered, grunted in satisfaction, then began to move with sure, heady strokes, drawing whimpers of need with each thrust.

High colour scoured his cheeks and a harshly beautiful face etched in fierce arousal filled her vision as she began to climb towards that spellbinding crest. Before enchantment completely consumed her, Saffie caressed and kissed everywhere she could reach, greedily tucking away sensation for later, when she could relive this experience from memory.

Shaky fingers traced his cheekbones, the mouth that could wreak such sweet chaos, and when he turned his head and kissed her palm, she felt her eyes prickle with tears.

It was too much.

He was too much.

Yet she couldn't stop it. Had no intention of

doing anything but surrendering to this unique feeling.

When she finally crested the peak, when there was nowhere to go but over that blissful edge, Saffie wrapped her arms tight around him, the only solid thing in her free-falling universe.

Beyond the wild rush of her climax, she heard him mutter in terse Portuguese before his movements grew uncoordinated, the force of his own climax drawing harsh grunts from his throat.

For several minutes only the frenzied sounds of their breathing echoed in the vast bedroom.

Then Joao rolled over, taking her with him and sprawling her over his large body. Long fingers combed through her hair, smoothing it back from her sweat-dampened forehead.

Saffie kept her eyes closed, the hypnotic pounding of his heartbeat lulling her into post-coital drowsiness. But it wasn't enough to fall asleep. Nor did she want to. She didn't want to miss a second of this out-of-time experience.

When his hand made another pass over her face, she caught a glimpse of his scar and her heart lurched. Aware she was treading on dangerous territory but unable to stop herself, she caught his hand in hers, traced her finger along the long white mark, then braved his gaze.

'How did you get this scar?'

CHAPTER SEVEN

JOAO TENSED AT the question, everything inside him freezing at the subject he didn't want to broach. He didn't want to be pitied. Nor did he want to leave himself vulnerable to exposition. Or gossip.

Hadn't many of his lovers asked the same question, their eyes brimming with curiosity, while their carefully crafted concerns hid more salacious intentions of what they could do with post-sex pillow talk?

Not once had he given them the satisfaction.

But Saffie was different. In the past four years, not once had she broken his confidence.

Except…this was *personal*.

And what they'd just done? His seed currently growing in her belly? Did it get any more personal than that?

He caught her wandering finger, stared down at her when she gave a soft gasp, but saw nothing but open, unsullied curiosity.

That need to unburden struck him hard again.

Deus, what was happening to him?

Her eyes began to dim, her expression growing wary at his silence.

He exhaled. 'You remember when I told you my mother was a drug addict?' he said, noting his strained tone.

She nodded.

'Well, if there was anything left over after she was done shooting up, she considered buying food for her son. If there wasn't…' He shrugged. 'Let's just say that the moment I learned to talk and reason for myself I was left to my own devices.'

Her eyes softened with sympathy. 'Joao.'

He swallowed a curious lump in his throat and fought the need to bury his face in her throat, inhale her very essence.

'Did you see much of her before she died?'

'No. She severed the umbilical permanently when I turned ten years old.'

Saffie raised her head, pain patent in her eyes. 'She left when you were that young?'

He pressed his lips together. '*Sim*. Much like you were,' he murmured, finding it strangely comforting that they had that in common.

Her lovely eyes shadowed. 'But you knew your parents. I…never knew mine.'

'Consider yourself lucky, then.'

'Well, I don't,' she said sharply, then took a deep breath. 'Maybe knowing and enduring what you did feels like the worst torture—'

Joao couldn't help his derisive snort.

She pressed on regardless. 'But not knowing where you came from or why you were abandoned on a park bench with a note that said you were better off without your mother is also a hell of its own, trust me.'

Trust me. A dart of discomfort pierced him.

As a rule he didn't trust anyone. That had served him well. Not trusting meant no one could let him down.

'Did you ever attempt to locate your mother?'

Her eyes grew darker and something twisted inside Joao. He wanted to take her pain away, he realised with a stark, sharp kind of clarity.

'I spent the better part of a year's salary chasing leads that went nowhere,' she said. 'But then I realised she never tried to find me either, so perhaps I needed to honour her wishes and stay away.'

'And you're satisfied with not knowing? With honouring the wishes of a woman who made the choices she made?'

He was aware his tone was harsh but she shrugged. 'I have to be. It hurt for a long time but

I can't blame her when I don't know the whole story.'

'How very magnanimous of you,' he said dryly.

'Maybe it was, maybe it wasn't. I just knew I had to find a way to be okay with it for my sanity's sake. Besides, I promised my foster mother I would look forwards instead of in the past.'

He had no answer to that, nor could he fault her for it. After all, he'd had to find his own way to contain the bitterness and pain, to rise above it in order to move forward. But he was aware it was very much a part of him, that most times it fuelled his ambition. For a moment he envied Saffie her simple circumspection. Her acceptance. Her willingness to create something… unique from her experiences.

Joao realised his hand had wandered over her belly, was stroking the smooth skin beneath which his seed grew. That pulse of ownership returned, stronger than ever.

'But that doesn't explain how you got this, though.' She brushed her fingers across his palm once again.

He shuddered, partly from her seductive touch, partly from memories he couldn't avoid any longer.

'I spent the better part of my youth running away from gangs. In the *favela* you were either with a gang or against them all. When things got desperate I joined one for a few weeks but I always drew the line when they tried to get me to sell drugs or rob tourists.' He stopped, his heart thudding as he stared at the scar. 'One particular gang leader didn't take kindly to me joining up just to get something to eat and then disappearing. He found me and decided to teach me a lesson.'

Saffie gasped in horror. 'By cutting your hand?'

He smiled grimly. 'His intention was to cut off a few fingers. He didn't get the chance to finish the job.'

'How... Who stopped him?'

'*Um anjo negro*, if you believe in that sort of thing.'

'A dark...angel?' she translated hesitantly.

Joao smiled, a curious pulse of satisfaction hitting him in the chest. 'Your Portuguese is improving, *querida*.'

She gave a shy smile. 'Who was he?'

'I discovered later that he was a doctor attached to an international charity, which was fortunate because after he saved me, I ran away without thanking him. But when I developed an infection, I went to find him. He made a deal with me. I would clean his house and tend his garden and in return he would give me an education, free of charge.'

'And that's how…?'

Joao nodded. 'He started me off with the basics and when he saw how quickly I picked up the subjects, he hired a tutor for me. I was able to take the requisite exams to get myself into university in record time. When I graduated he gave me the capital I needed to invest in my first business.'

Her eyes widened. 'My God, Joao, that's amazing.'

He wanted to bask in her joy. God, he wanted to do more than that, and that forceful swell of need was what froze everything inside him.

He couldn't *need* like that again.

It came too close to the fervent prayers of a lost little boy who'd sent up hundreds of pleas to the cosmos only to be answered with stony silence. He'd learned to rely on no one but himself. And he'd succeeded.

There could be no turning back, no opening himself up to vulnerabilities. So he crafted a passable smile and shrugged. 'Like with everything else, I paid the price by earning my keep and turning failure into success. The good doctor has been repaid a hundred times over for his generosity. That's all there really is to it.'

The light in her eyes dimmed. 'Surely you don't really believe that?'

'What else is there?'

'That he saw something special in you, that you were more than just a simple project to him? Maybe he was trying to give you what your own father didn't?'

Ernesto Blanco had been a slave-driver, true. But there'd also been times when he'd just wanted to…talk. Find out Joao's hopes and dreams. Joao had ensured he'd curtailed those occurrences.

Because…where was the sense in opening himself up only to be disappointed? To be discarded and made to feel worthless and inconsequential?

Now an arrow of guilt lanced him, unfreezing him enough to make him glance down at Saffie.

'That was a long time ago. It doesn't matter now.' Just as he hadn't done with Ernesto, he saw no point in delving into his *feelings* with Saffie.

This way would ensure they didn't stray from their synergy.

But as she slowly laid her head on his chest, her fist curled in a ball against his skin, Joao wondered why that reaction didn't please him.

Why there was suddenly a hollow space where supreme satisfaction had reigned so majestically before.

The only answer that came to him, he totally rejected.

Because Joao Oliviera didn't *need* anyone. And he most certainly didn't yearn for feelings that were as ephemeral as snow in summer.

Saffron awoke with the sinking feeling that deepened in the minutes she wasted staring up at the high, crown-moulded ceilings in Joao's master suite.

She'd felt him leave the bed an hour ago and had pretended to be asleep. The predominantly cowardly part of her hadn't wanted to face him, see the regret she'd heard in his voice at the tail end of their conversation last night, transmitted to what had happened in bed. She already knew he regretted opening up his past to her. She'd seen it in his eyes before sleep had pulled her under.

The irony wasn't lost on her that she'd told herself this was a one-night-only thing, only to find she didn't want it to be for Joao.

She'd intended to indulge in the physical, only to end up feeling closer to the man he'd unveiled last night, the strength of character needed to overcome his adversities striking at her emotions, forcing her to admit what her heart already knew. He was special. And she wanted more from him.

Her hand cradled her belly, her heart tumbling over as she accepted the truth.

She wanted more than the children he'd made with her.

This not so secret yearning was the reason she'd talked herself out of leaving his employment all these years. It was the reason she'd agreed to another three months with him when she should've walked away.

Panic momentarily engulfed her at the admission.

But now that she knew the danger she was facing, could she halt her feelings? Accept that Joao would never feel that way towards her and carry on with her life without stepping into the pitfalls?

Even as she pondered it, she knew she was grasping at straws. Being around him, witnessing his intellectual brilliance and dangerous charm was what had led to her sleeping with him in Morocco.

But even knowing and fearing for her emotional well-being, was she prepared to walk away?

And what about his vow to lay claim on the babies she carried?

A knock came at the door, thankfully giving

her the excuse to put aside her churning thoughts. She answered, her spirits dropping further because Joao wouldn't knock at his own door.

The butler entered, bearing a tray. Accepting it, Saffie asked, 'Is Mr Oliviera here?'

'He asked me to inform you that he was attending an early-morning meeting. That he'll see you at the office at lunchtime. You were to take your time this morning,' he delivered with a smile.

He wasn't sidelining her, she knew that. He often gave her part of the morning off after a big event, especially if there were meetings he could attend solo.

Still, her heart dropped.

He couldn't have sent a clearer message than to leave her alone in his bed the morning after their night together. She'd pried into his private life, he'd given her the answers she wanted. And was now distancing himself.

That distance bled into their second week in Shanghai.

They remained in complete synergy workwise and, in every other way, he treated her with cool professionalism.

Out of the office was a different matter. At events where she was required to accompany him—an occurrence which seemed to have suddenly tripled—Joao took every opportunity to make physical contact. He pulled her close when her attention wandered, took her hand when they happened to be at whatever red-carpet event, and he was required to interact with the media, and danced with her at every gala or fundraiser.

All without engaging her in anything more than perfunctory conversation beyond complimenting her on how she looked, asking about the state of her morning sickness.

All while making contact with some part of her body.

Her hand. Her face. Her hair. Her hip.

Saffie was completely tortured by it.

By the time they arrived in Sao Paolo a gruelling seven days later, after a brief stopover in London, Saffie was thoroughly sick of it.

So it was with gritted teeth that she stepped off the plane the next Saturday. The SUV that would drive them a short distance to the helicopter taking them to Joao's estate idled a few yards away. As she dashed for it, her right wedge heel twisted.

'Atento!' Joao grasped her arm and steadied her. *'Deus*, if I didn't know better, I would think you were trying to get away from me.'

'And you would be right!'

He slid in beside her, his gaze coolly speculative as he slammed the door and reached for her seat belt.

'Care to tell me what's bothering you?'

She grabbed the belt from him and secured it herself, then immediately wished she'd worn her hair in its customary bun instead of brushed out and loose, when it got in her way. She reached up to flick the offending strand away but he beat her to it, his fingers slowly threading through her hair before tucking it behind her ear.

Her heart flip-flopped in an erratic rhythm when his fingers lingered on her neck before drawing away. 'What exactly are you playing at, Joao?' she asked abruptly. A little desperately.

'Be concise with your questions, *por favor*,' he rasped as the vehicle rolled for half a mile to stop next to another gleaming aircraft.

'When we're in the office you barely speak to me except to issue orders. And yet when we're in company you won't stop...*touching* me. You treat me like I'm some attention-seeking pet. And frankly I'm sick of it.'

She stopped, realised her breathing was as fitful as her heartbeat and her face was burning with what must be high colour.

Beside her, Joao stiffened. 'I wasn't aware my touch was so offensive.'

It isn't.

Saffie was fiercely glad her pursed lips stopped the words from spilling free. But the task of holding them in caused another tremor to course through her body.

He saw her reaction, and his face grew tauter. 'Perhaps, for the sake of avoiding hyperventilation, we should discuss this when we reach our destination?' he quipped coolly with one spiked eyebrow.

'I'm quite capable of having a civilised conversation.'

'I beg to differ. You seem quite worked up about…whatever is on your mind.'

She opened her mouth to contradict him but he was alighting, holding his hand out to her while his gaze dared her to refuse. She knew it wasn't beyond him to transfer her bodily from SUV to helicopter, so she let him assist her.

Minutes later, they were airborne. And since this particular chopper provided no privacy, Saffie had to hold her tongue as they flew over stunning skyscrapers in the heart of Sao Paolo, then tightly packed and precariously stacked concrete housing that constituted the dirt-poor *favelas*.

Momentarily, Saffie curbed her own angst in the face of such deprivation, and when her gaze flicked to Joao, he was staring down, too, his face frozen tight.

Did you grow up here? she wanted to ask. But she didn't want to invade his privacy just to satisfy her curiosity. Perhaps he caught the question in her eyes when his head swivelled towards her because he shook his head.

'One *favela* looks pretty much like another but the place of my birth is a little further away, nearer Rio.'

The bleakness in his voice made her want to throw her arms around him, but if these past three weeks had taught her anything, it was that she liked bodily contact with Joao a little too much.

Which was why she was fighting his careless caresses. It was that or go mad or, worse, beg him to never stop.

The *favelas* gave way to a lusher landscape, stretching for miles in every direction. She'd been to Joao's estate in Rio but not to this one. Unable to stem her anticipation, she leaned forward.

The giant shape of a white stallion etched into the side of a hill was breathtaking. It was Joao's personal crest and was stamped on every piece of stationery and property he owned.

They soared over rambling stables and open fields where stallions raced across the grass. Over giant gazebos and *churrascaria* pits smoking prime meats. Over cattle grazing on endless pampas to one side, and tennis courts, and not one but four separate summerhouses attached to Olympic-sized swimming pools on the other.

Then, past stylishly tiered, beautiful landscaped lawns, they soared over a sprawling red-roofed villa with several interconnecting wings that looked as if several properties had been artistically fused into one.

Her lips were still parted in awe when they landed on a designated helipad.

Saffie stepped out to a soft breeze that ruffled her hair.

Joao glanced over when she reached up to secure it, his lips pursed.

By the time they made the short trip up the steps to one of many entrances to the house, two dozen staff were lined up, all wearing pristine uniforms with a discreet stallion logo pressed into their nameplates.

Joao greeted them in his native tongue, then glanced at Saffie. 'These are the core staff you'll need to work with to prepare for Lavinia's arrival. You know how many staff work here, so if you need more just consult with the head housekeeper.'

At the last count, she knew they numbered seventy-five, just to take care of the villa and the grounds. 'Do all the staff live on the estate?' she asked as he stepped into a *salon* that looked as if it belonged in the pages of a glossy magazine.

'Like with the executive condos, I provide extensive housing to all my top staff. I believe it's easier that way.'

And as perks went, they were second to none. Saffie knew it was why Joao remained the number one desired boss to work for. But she was beginning to think it was more than that. 'Easier or because you want to make a bigger difference in their lives?' she asked before she could stop herself.

He froze in the middle of one of the many hallways that branched off into the villa.

'Are you attempting to romanticise my actions, Saffie?' he queried with a quiet, softly dangerous tone that filled every pore of her skin as surely as his body filled her vision.

Behind him a painting she very much suspected was an original Mondrian failed to hold her attention because the man staring at her was a masterpiece head and shoulders above all others.

He was even more to her, and to so many. Did he see that? Or was he blind to it all? 'You said you wanted to teach your… Pueblo that he was wrong to make himself your enemy. But you're so much more than one man's opinion of you, Joao. I've seen people react to shallow, selfish rich folks who throw their money around. That's not what I see with those who work for you. I've also seen the company poll. Do you know how many people said they would work for you even if you cut their salary in half?'

For the briefest moment, he looked mildly shocked, shaken even. Then his mouth tightened. 'I'm not exactly sure where you're going with this but let me assure you of one thing. I'm no one's knight in shining armour,' he answered tersely.

The slight quake in her body sent her fingers to her hair only to recall it wasn't in a bun. 'Just because you don't want the prize doesn't mean it doesn't belong to you,' she muttered.

Joao's gaze dropped from where he'd been watching her toy with her hair. For several seconds, he didn't breathe, only watched her with something akin to bewilderment. Then abruptly, he stepped back. 'I have a few calls to make. Since you seem to have a bee in your bonnet about my presence, I'm sure you'll welcome the chance to rest and explore on your own.'

He started to walk away.

'No, I won't,' she said firmly.

* * *

Joao knew he should walk away. That the simmering emotions that had left him far from calm since their night in Shanghai were in serious danger of erupting.

'Excuse me?' The question was just to buy himself time, straighten thoughts that lately scattered in her presence.

But nothing seemed to be working. She'd burrowed deep inside him to a point where his thoughts started and ended with Saffie. As for that hard-core masochism he'd developed where the need to touch her felt as vital as breathing? He silently shook his head.

Like an addict, he'd known he was courting trouble. But again, he'd found justification for it. More public appearances with Saffie…just so he had an excuse to touch her without falling foul of their agreement in Shanghai. Just so he could allay his dread at the thought of her leaving. As if touching her, making sure she was by his side, was all he needed at any given time.

He still desired her. And even before their night together was over, he knew it would never be enough. That he should've negotiated for more.

But they'd agreed. And he'd left his bed the next morning knowing he'd rather she stayed by his side, as his assistant, than left because he wanted her in his bed with a fever that consumed him.

Saffie shrugged. 'Thanks to your actions, the world seems to think we're either about to or already are sleeping together. I don't want to *rest* and I don't want to *explore* or do anything until you explain to me why you've been acting as if I belong to you when we're in public.'

Since that was exactly what he'd been doing, Joao experienced a pang of guilt. One which he immediately justified. 'You mean beyond sending out a clear message that I won't welcome my assistant being poached?'

Anger and a touch of disappointment flitted across her face. 'Don't take me for a fool, Joao. That message could've been relayed with a few words from you like you did with Will Ashby in Shanghai.'

He padded back to where she stood, fighting the temptation to touch her. When the warmth of her body called temptingly to his.

But even as he tried to talk himself down, his hand rose, hovered over skin so smooth and alluring he felt his heart flip over. Only by flattening it against the wall beside her head, and gritting his teeth, did he stop the urge.

Saffie tilted her head, boldly met his eyes, demanding an answer without the faintest knowledge that she set his emotions aflame with a simple look. Or did she know? She'd made herself indispensable in one area of his life. Was she making herself indispensable in that part of his life he'd never let anyone else?

She licked her bottom lip, a nervous action that left him far too weak and far too vulnerable for his liking.

Again, he knew he should walk away. And yet he found himself answering.

'You wish to know why?' he asked after several, pulse-destroying seconds had passed. 'I'm trying to understand you, Saffie. I'm trying to see beneath the insane need to the *why.*'

Her delicate nostrils pinched. 'Why what?'

'Why I expose things to you that no one else knows. Why lately I tolerate your mild insubordination and you delving into matters that don't concern you when I would've fired others on the spot. Why I can't stop you from getting under my skin,' he breathed.

Her eyes darkened and a slight tremor went through her. He yearned to explore that reaction but he knew he was already skating on the edge. From that moment he'd confessed he needed her, his world had tilted on its axis. That visceral confession seemed to be one he couldn't take back no matter how hard he tried.

'It still doesn't explain why you touch me, Joao.'

The breath expelled from his lungs; he watched it ruffle the soft hair at her temple and once again fought the desire to touch her. 'Do I need to spell it out? I still desire you. But we agreed on one night, and I don't want to give you an excuse to walk away.' He gave a short, self-deprecating laugh. 'But you needn't worry. I may have let myself get carried away but I don't intend to act on it.'

She licked her lips, and the simmer turned into a torrent. 'Do I want to know the reasons behind that conclusion?'

A sliver of ice cut through the heat, scalpel-sharp and reopening wounds he believed long decayed. 'Because blind lust jeopardises everything. My father had a wife and children of his own at home, and yet he repeatedly gave into weakness, which led to my unwanted birth. And then he spent a significant amount of time attempting to diminish my existence. *We* gave into blind lust, too, didn't we? Look where we are.'

Sharp lacerations bloodied her heart and for a moment Saffie couldn't breathe through the pain to tell him he was wrong. That he was a far better man than his father could ever hope to be. That Shanghai wasn't a mistake for her.

He placed one long finger over her lips before she could respond. 'No need for more protest. I know where I stand. And you were right when you said this needed to stop.' He dropped his hand and stepped back. 'You won't need to suffer my touch any longer.'

With that, he strode away.

She was still there, her heart thudding dully in her chest, when Rubinho, the head butler, found her.

'Would madam like some refreshments in the salon or in her suite?' the young man asked.

She tried to focus beyond her deafening despair. 'I… My suite would be fine.'

He nodded briskly. 'Allow me to escort you to the south wing, *por favor.*'

She followed on wooden feet through several more stunning hallways and sweeping staircases.

Villa Sábia was magnificent in a way that awed and lifted the most depleted spirit. And Saffie was no less immune to the magic of the sprawling estate as she took in the authentic Brazilian architecture, the ethnic woodwork and international objets d'art that had gone into making the property one of the most stunning in the world.

By the time they approached the hallway that led to the south wing, she understood why she'd fended off numerous requests from top magazines to photograph Joao's home.

Style, luxury, elegance, comfort. There wasn't one piece of furniture or art that didn't seamlessly elevate the true beauty of the villa. Not a surface she didn't want to caress or just stand and admire in awe.

Her suite was no exception. And she wasn't surprised when her love of Joao's villa directly fused with her dangerously emotional sentiments for the man himself.

She knew it might be a futile attempt but she tried to counteract it by immersing herself in her own work. An hour after arrival she'd forced herself to eat a light tapas meal, after which she'd met with the senior household staff to discuss menus, wine and the guest list for the reception dinner planned in Lavinia's honour the next night.

Afterwards, she was going through her diary when a reminder pinged that made her breath catch.

She'd officially reached the end of her first trimester yesterday. Her morning sickness had passed but Joao still insisted on the doctor accompanying them on their trips.

The same doctor would be conducting another health check tomorrow morning, including the ultrasound. Her heart skipped a beat, swelling with a love almost impossible to contain.

Everything she'd wanted was nestled in her womb.

Almost everything...

And she would have to be content with that because Joao had made his stance clear. He might desire her, but the emotional risk wasn't worth taking for him. Perhaps he even secretly couldn't wait to see the back of her once she'd fulfilled her usefulness on the Archer deal?

The stark agony that accompanied that realisation made her set her tablet aside. Shakily, she walked to the edge of the large terrace she'd chosen for her meeting. Beyond three tiers of landscaped garden and off the right of a trellised gazebo she saw the largest of the four swimming pools, sparkling in the late-afternoon sun.

She had two free hours before dinner and, eager to occupy herself with something other than her anguishing thoughts, she hurried to her suite and changed into a swimsuit.

The bra cups of her bikini felt a little snug and she avoided looking at herself in the mirror as she secured the ties. She hadn't had time to buy new ones, so they'd just have to do.

Throwing on a silk beach robe, she fished out

her sunglasses and sun cream and headed downstairs.

At the poolside, Saffie discarded her robe and stood on the edge of the pool, her face lifted up to the warm sun, wishing she could blank her mind of the anxiety for just a minute. Or, failing that, wishing she had a crystal ball to see into a future where she was fully content with just her and her babies.

Where the absence of Joao didn't cut her like a knife.

Shaking her head free of fairy tales, Saffie lowered herself into the pool. She swam lazy laps, the joy of the cool water washing over her soothing her senses, until thirst drove her out. After drinking half a glass of her lime-based punch, delivered while she'd been in the water, she returned to sit on the wide shallow steps of the pool, her feet in the water.

Then, as so often happened in her quiet moments, her mind went to the babies growing within her.

Her breath caught softly.

Twins.

Double the love. Double the joy. Her hand glided over her stomach as her eyes drifted shut and momentary sadness overwhelmed her. She would've given anything for her foster mother to have been alive, to share her happiness.

The letter from her foster mother, written in the last weeks of her life, the one Saffie kept between the pages of her childhood diary but knew every word of, flipped through her mind.

Don't dwell on the past.
Find your own happiness.
Never settle for loneliness.

I'm almost there, she said softly under her breath. But I think I need more, Mum, her heart defiantly added.

As if he were configured by her imagination, her skin began to tingle with hyperawareness that only came with Joao's presence.

The shape of that *more.*

'Saffie.' Her name was a warm, deep throb.

Breath snagged in her throat, she opened her eyes to find him a few feet away. His gaze was riveted on the hand on her stomach, a depth of emotion she'd never seen before blazing in his eyes.

Her fingers spread, an instinctive awareness of her womanhood that came out of nowhere. 'Joao. Did you want something?'

'*Sim*, I do.' His gaze didn't rise from her belly but he continued to speak. 'The Brazilian sun isn't one you want to underestimate. Did you put any sunscreen on when you came out here?'

She swallowed, not because of the question but because in all their time together she'd never seen Joao clad in all white. The effect of the white linen trousers that sat low on his hips and the unbuttoned white linen shirt threw his vibrant olive complexion into stunning relief. When that was topped with his slightly dishevelled hair, whisky-gold eyes and the faint stubble caressing his jaw, Saffie was in danger of being completely overwhelmed by his presence. 'I was going to swim again before—'

He made an impatient sound under his breath before striding over to grab the sunscreen bottle she'd left on the table between two loungers.

Without care for his clothes, Joao returned and brazenly waded into the pool. One step up from where she sat, he took up position behind her and flipped open the lid of the bottle.

'What are you doing?' she asked breathlessly.

'Helping you avoid sunburn. Lift your hair out of the way, Saffie,' he ordered, his tone a husky rasp that wrecked havoc with her equilibrium.

Caught under a spell she couldn't, and secretly didn't want to, extricate herself from, she sat up straighter, one hand on her belly while the other twisted her hair in a rope and held it up.

Beyond her peripheral vision a bee buzzed, and the earthy, smoky scent of *churrascaria* fire teased the air. Samba music played faintly in the background. But all Saffie could concentrate on was the powerful frame bracketing hers, the smooth exhalations teasing the wispy hairs at her nape.

The combination of the cool cream and warm fingers made her bite back a gasp, then fight harder to suppress a moan as his hand glided in firm strokes across her shoulders. Between one breath and the next, the atmosphere around them thickened, the only sound their arrhythmic breathing and the gentle susurration of the sparkling pool.

Saffie swallowed when both hands moved over her upper back. Back and forth in a seductive dance that made her thighs clench, made her squeeze her eyes shut as need clamoured dizzyingly through her.

Joao encountered the string at her back and gave an impatient grunt. 'I'm going to untie this,' he said in a low, deep voice, his breath brushing her earlobe and sending a fresh shiver through her. 'The staff are discreet. You won't be seen. Okay?'

The sound she made under her breath was pathetically weak but he took it for the assent it was and tugged the strings free.

The wicked combination of damp, loosened material and his expert touch instantaneously stiffened her sensitive nipples into hard, needy peaks.

Behind her, Joao exhaled harshly as his hands moved down her waist to the small of her back, then around to brush her hand away before gliding over her midriff and belly.

The doctor had warned her that with twins she would start to show very soon, and over the last few days a definite bump had appeared, and with it the wondrous ability to take her breath away simply by looking down at her belly.

'Você é tão bonita,' he whispered under his breath, almost to himself as he caressed the taut skin of her belly.

But she heard. And understood.

You are so beautiful.

She started to turn towards him. 'Joao…' The sudden urge to cover his hand with hers blossomed but before she could give into the insanity, his fingers moved up to the lower curve of her heavy breasts.

This time she couldn't smother her moan or stop her head from lolling back against his shoulder.

Joao exhaled heavily, then his hands moved behind her to secure the ties again. *'Cristo, isso é loucura,'* he muttered tersely under his breath.

No, he wasn't the only one going insane.

'I trust you can take care of the rest?' he growled in her ear.

She gave a jerky little nod but his hand lingered for a pulse-thumping five seconds before he stood up abruptly, his feet splashing lightly as he stepped out of the pool.

'Don't stay out here too long. I've asked for dinner to be served at seven.'

Saffie nodded again, then forced herself to remain still, knowing that if she turned and faced him, if she so much as caught a glint of hunger in his eyes she would do the unthinkable and beg him to sweep her off her feet, carry her to his bed and make love to her.

Several minutes after he'd left, she remained in the throes of sensation, her oversensitive body unwilling to release her from Joao's all-powerful thrall.

But it was more than that. Saffie knew the problem was her heart and the unstoppable yearning growing with each second.

Just as she knew she had to find a solution soon…before she reached the dreaded point of no return.

* * *

The dress she chose for dinner was a stylish one-shouldered below-the-knee design that clung to her breasts and hips. The soft cotton accentuated her slight bump and she caught Joao's gaze on her belly when she arrived in the living room.

He waved the butler away and pulled out her chair, his gaze lingering over her throat and bare arms as he retook his seat. 'No signs of a burn?'

'None at all,' she replied with a forced lightness.

By silent mutual agreement, they made light, business conversation, choosing not to discuss the sensually charged scene at the pool.

'You think Lavinia will enjoy the soccer match?'

His lips compressed before he swallowed a mouthful of the exclusive Oliviera red burgundy he enjoyed with his steaks. 'My teams aren't at the top of the national and international leagues for nothing,' he stated with the casual arrogance of man who knew the kind of power and influence he wielded.

After purchasing his first Brasileirãoclub, Clube de Magdalena Santina, he'd spent millions seducing top players from around the world to his team. They'd immediately started winning trophies, the most prized of which currently sitting on a mantel in Joao's Rio de Janeiro villa.

'And the team they're playing against tomorrow?'

'Below us in the championship. Where they belong,' he added with a hardened edge of satisfaction.

The curious answer triggered a memory. 'That's your father's team, isn't it?'

'Sim,' he confirmed with a grim smile.

'Is he going to be there tomorrow?'

He rolled the stem of his glass between long fingers. 'I should think so.'

Enlightenment widened her eyes. 'You knew he was, that's why you wanted Lavinia to be there.'

Joao shrugged. 'I thought it was time to stop dancing around her decision and make her face us once and for all. Everything is in place, I trust?'

'Of course.'

He picked up his glass in a silent toast. *'Bom.* Here's to all our hard work paying off.'

CHAPTER EIGHT

S<small>UNDAY DAWNED BRIGHT</small> and glorious.

Having taken advantage of the king-size bed on Joao's private jet, Saffie found the effects of jet lag were minimal, which helped a little with her frame of mind as she took a long, luxurious shower and dressed for breakfast.

The flared white halter-neck dress swung soothingly around her knees as she left her suite.

Carlotta, Joao's deputy housekeeper, met her at the bottom of the stairs and smilingly led her through another series of hallways to a vast courtyard overlooking the second largest swimming pool on the estate.

Joao was already seated, lazily flicking through a Portuguese newspaper. He lowered it as she approached, his gaze hooded as it rested on her face.

'*Bom dia.* Did you sleep well?'

'*Sim, obrigado.*'

One corner of his mouth lifted, unmistakeable satisfaction framing his smile. 'You're making good strides with your Portuguese. Soon you'll be more fluent than I am.'

'You're much too competitive to hand me that advantage.'

A shadow passed over his face but he didn't comment, instead offering her the fruit platter, and nodding at the butler, who stepped forward to fill her cup with aromatic tea.

Calmly, he went back to his paper, leaving her to wonder what she'd said to garner that reaction.

She was almost done with breakfast when Carlotta stepped onto the terrace. '*Senhor*, the doctor is here. We have set him up in the Redondo Suite, as instructed,' she said in slightly accented English.

He thanked her and rose. 'Shall we?'

She remained seated. 'Has something happened? You seem to be…in a mood.'

His lips twisted. 'Do I?'

She pressed her lips together, then decided to forge ahead with the elephant in the room. 'If it's about what happened by the pool yesterday—'

'That was a mistake,' he interrupted with calm precision. 'But perhaps it's precipitated the need for a few changes.'

Her heart plummeted. 'What kind of changes?' she asked with a voice that tasted ashen.

Joao hesitated. 'Necessary changes we'll discuss after the Archer deal is put to bed. One that might mean I remain here in Brazil.'

He was planning to stay in Brazil without her?

She felt the colour drain from her face, her windpipe squeezing alarmingly. 'What…exactly are you saying?'

'The doctor's waiting, Saffie. Let's not get drawn into protracted conversations.'

She wanted to remind him that he was Joao Oliviera. That he called shots in his sleep and grown men jumped. But he was already stepping behind her chair, pointedly urging her into movement.

The Redondo Suite was exactly as described, a circular guest suite with spectacular views and breathtaking murals etched into its dome-like ceiling. The Brazilian doctor who'd travelled with them from London greeted them and efficiently set up the machine.

Within minutes, the sound of twin heartbeats filled the room.

Between Shanghai and London, Joao had ordered the most sophisticated ultrasound machine and Saffie's breath caught as the 3D image of her still-forming babies loomed large.

'Their growth chart is excellent. Well within the expected parameters,' the doctor said. 'Your babies are doing fine.'

She chanced a glance at where Joao sat at the end of her bed, his thigh brushing her knee. He was staring transfixed at the screen, his throat working. A moment later, his gaze shifted to her stomach, and when it flicked up to meet hers, his expression was awed.

He isn't unaffected, her brain screeched loudly. *This isn't just a blind asset-claiming for him.*

Her heart started to hammer for a completely different, breathtaking reason. Did she dare hope for more? Should she risk telling him she was considering staying beyond three months?

'While it's still a little early, I can hazard a guess as to the sex of the babies if either of you wish to know?'

'They are healthy. That's all that matters,' Joao said.

But Saffie shook her head. 'I want to know, please. I can't stand the suspense.'

The doctor smiled. 'There's a strong likelihood that you're expecting twin boys.'

Joao inhaled sharply, his face tightening with raw, unfettered emotion before the mask slid back into place. His hand rose to hover beside her. After a moment he swallowed and dropped it back down.

And just like that, wild hope turned to dust.

She kept her gaze firmly fixed on the doctor for the remainder of the examination, and breathed with strained relief when it was over.

As Joao escorted him out, the sound of rotor blades filled the air.

Lavinia's arrival forestalled any private interaction with Joao, a fact Saffie wasn't sure whether to be pleased or further agonised about.

The older woman, bright-eyed and raring to go, promptly demanded an extensive tour of the estate.

In the custom-made air-conditioned buggy, Saffie caught Lavinia's subtle questions, probing Joao's values and intentions.

As she listened to him field them with a dextrous mix of charm and intellect, Saffie also realised one thing.

While Joao might be locked in battle with his father and was bitter about his upbringing, it hadn't diminished the part of him that selflessly provided for those in need or gave back to people who served him. He could have easily become selfish and close-minded over his start in life. But he'd done the opposite. He'd provided jobs to a staggering amount of Brazilians, invested in organic, self-sustaining ventures that were the envy of most organisations, and there was the unabashed pride in his heritage that throbbed in his voice when he spoke of his country.

She'd known he was a man of integrity from her first professional interaction with him.

And as their helicopter came in to land in the middle of the football stadium that held one hundred and twenty thousand screaming soccer fans chanting Joao's name, Saffie knew there was no point talking herself out of the inevitable because it'd already happened.

She was in love with Joao Oliviera.

The earth-shaking admission both terrified and thrilled her. She placed a balled fist against her heart, as if it would stop its reckless pounding.

'What's wrong?' The question was sharp.

Startled, she realised that even while he'd greeted his players, introduced them to a goggle-eyed Lavinia, and acknowledged the crowd, he'd kept an eye on her.

She hurriedly composed her features. 'Nothing. The crowd's a little overwhelming, that's all.'

He nodded tersely. 'Then we will retire to somewhere more private. Come.'

He held out his arm to her, his gaze enigmatic as he watched her. She was reminded of their conversation and his promise that he wouldn't touch her, and her heart skipped a beat. But the moment she took his arm, he held out the other to Lavinia, disavowing her of the notion that it was anything other than simple courtesy, and led them off the red carpet laid out especially for him on the field.

The immense owner's box granting unfettered access to the field was decked with twenty-five sumptuous luxury leather seats, while on the tables vintage champagne, oysters, caviar and other glorious canapés teased every appetite.

After introductions were made to the mayor and several dignitaries, Saffie left Joao to further dazzle Lavinia and took a seat as the countdown to kick-off began.

But even removed from the power gathering, she couldn't stop her gaze from devouring Joao's stunning male beauty, from wondering when it'd happened.

At what exact moment had her heart decided to risk everything by falling in love with her boss?

What did it matter?

It was done. Her heart belonged to him.

The only problem was, did he want it? Now or ever? Or was that promise of distance just the beginning of a chasm she might not be able to breach?

Her heart dropped, her fingers clenching painfully at the searing truth that she might have to.

That the cardinal sin of falling in love with an unattainable man might be her undoing.

A throat cleared beside her. Again, Saffron startled, heat rushing to her face when she realised she'd been staring at Joao like a lovelorn fool, probably projecting her feelings to the world.

The middle-aged man staring at her had hard features born of harsh living, but surprisingly kind, shrewd eyes.

'I don't believe we were introduced, probably because I arrived late. I'm Ernesto Blanco.'

Memory fell into place, and her breath caught. 'You're Joao's mentor.'

His brown eyes widened fractionally as he held out his hand. 'I'm not sure whether to be surprised you know about me or astonished that Joao used that term for our relationship.'

She thought it best not to mention that Joao hadn't. 'I'm Saffron Everhart.'

'*Sim*, the assistant worth her weight in gold.'

'Now it's my turn to be surprised.'

'Because you don't think you are?'

She shrugged. 'Because you're aware of my existence but I didn't know about yours until… recently.'

Ernest tilted his beer bottle in Joao's direction. 'Ah, but isn't that very much like the man we both know? A grandmaster at compartmentalising?'

As if pulled by powerful magnets, her gaze swung to Joao. He was staring at her with an electric gaze that rooted her to the spot for several seconds before swinging to Ernesto.

'Perhaps not for much longer,' Ernesto murmured.

She dragged her gaze back to him. 'I don't know what you mean.'

'You will, soon enough,' he said with a cryptic smile.

Saffie knew Joao was approaching from the way every cell zinged to life.

Ernesto stood and the two men clasped hands in that sombre way men who knew each other's gravest experiences did.

But within the older man's eyes, she spotted quiet pride and affection, the kind Saffron had only felt for a brief, blessed period before she'd lost the only parent she'd ever known.

Her heart plummeted further.

If Joao hadn't accepted the love of the father figure who'd pulled him out of a dismal future, what hope did she have that he'd accept hers?

The two men engaged in a low-murmured conversation before Ernesto moved away and Joao's hypnotic eyes slid to her. He didn't speak, but his gaze slid over the loose, stylish knot she'd heaped her hair into, then lower to the diamond studs in her ears and the simple diamond chains at her throat and wrists, over the sky-blue flared sundress and matching platform shoes.

Every second that passed with his eyes on her made her feel *alive*. Vital.

So unbearably needy for an emotional connection.

In that moment she didn't want to contemplate a time when she would be deprived of even the sight of him. But just as she'd had to accept the diagnosis of her mother's illness, she had to make room for the fact that the love foolishly swelling inside with every breath she took might not find its rightful home.

The very thought threatened to shatter her into a thousand useless pieces.

Joao's hands suddenly gripped hers. 'You're pale, Saffie. Are you unwell?' he rasped with fierce urgency.

She hurriedly shook her head and tugged her hands from his. 'No, I'm fine. But…we need to have that talk. I'd prefer it to be sooner rather than later.'

A shot of apprehension clouded his narrowed eyes. 'Any reason for the sudden urgency?'

Yes, my heart is on the line.

'Call me overoptimistic but I think the Archer deal is yours so, really, I've fulfilled my end of the bargain, don't you agree?'

An undecipherable look crossed his face. '*Sim.* If that is what you prefer, we will talk later.'

Saffie forced a nod. 'Thank you.'

Joao led her to the front row. Beyond the panoramic windows, the band struck the first notes of the national anthem.

From the moment of kick-off, Joao's team displayed breathtaking skill. With Ernesto taking up the self-appointed mantle of explaining the intricacies of soccer to Lavinia, Joao was freed to fully immerse himself in the sport he loved, a fact that didn't seem to please the man in the adjacent owner's box.

When Saffie caught his gaze for a third time, she forced herself to examine him. A second later, she knew she was staring at Pueblo Oliviera.

Her gaze flew to Joao. He was staring at her, a grim little smile on lips.

'That's your father, isn't it?' she asked a little redundantly.

When Joao's gaze shifted to the man, it was as if he'd been hewn from ice. 'If you mean the man whose sperm sired me, then yes,' he rasped grimly. 'But he doesn't deserve the title you bestow on him and he never will.'

The final whistle was a sharp trill, breaking the tense atmosphere.

Lavinia turned to Joao, a wide smile on her face. 'That was incredible. Now I get the whole buzz around this game.'

Joao inclined his head, made the appropriate responses as celebratory champagne was served, but Saffie could cut the tension cloaking him with a scalpel.

It thickened unbearably when Pueblo Oliviera strolled uninvited into their box.

Conversation trailed off but Pueblo, a man in his late fifties with salt-and-pepper hair, and face and frame that unmistakeably resembled Joao's, was undaunted. He exchanged greetings with guests, then sauntered over to where Joao stood with Lavinia.

For several minutes, he ignored his son, while ingratiating himself with Lavinia. But even while the older woman smiled and remained gracious, her attention repeatedly strayed to Joao, seeking his input on the match, the wine in the region, his plans for Archer Cruise Liners, rumoured to be the investment she'd established her name on.

'I intend to keep it,' Joao answered. 'It's not

a secret that I have Greek shipbuilders on contract for my own liners. But I am prepared to rename it the Archer Oliviera Cruise Line, if you're amenable.'

The older woman gasped. 'You would do that?'

Joao nodded. 'You have my word. Which is more than I can say for some.'

Pueblo snorted. 'I suggest you wait until it's written in indelible ink before you believe him, Mrs Archer.'

'One thing your son has a reputation for, Mr Oliviera, is never breaking his word,' Saffron blurted before she could stop herself.

Beside her, Joao stiffened, but when she glanced at him, his face was woodenly neutral, his fixed stare on his father.

Pueblo's eyebrows slowly went up as he slid a scathing glance over Saffron. 'I see you have another eager woman racing to your defence,' he said, addressing his son for the first time. 'I thought I'd seen the last of that with your pathetic mother.'

Saffie's breath caught but Joao responded evenly. 'We both know she was doing that simply to score money for drugs. The question here is who is more deplorable for exploiting a drug addict in return for sex?'

Pueblo went red in the face, fury steaming

from him as he took a menacing step towards his son. His mouth worked but no words emerged.

'What precisely do you want to say to me?' Joao taunted icily. 'That I'm worthless? That I'll amount to nothing? Or that you've been proven wrong on your every prediction but still believe you hold the upper hand in the game?'

His father gave a scoffing laugh. 'You truly think you're better than me?'

Joao spread his arms wide and smirked. 'My achievements speak volumes for themselves.'

Either Pueblo Oliviera was too dense to see he was nowhere in his son's league or too proud to admit when he was beaten. Saffie suspected it was the latter.

'I was winning long before you were born,' he growled.

'And still you haven't learned your lesson, that all it takes is a little nurturing to make the difference between long-term success and instant gratification. I see what I want, I claim it and I *keep* it, while you grab then toss without seeing the value in anything.'

The flash of uncertainty briefly blunted Pueblo's fury. But a moment later, the older man's gaze flicked around the room, saw the audience he'd garnered.

Without a word, he turned on his heel and left, his small entourage trailing him.

The tight expression on Joao's face eased, enough for her to catch a glimpse of his agony. Unable to stop the visceral need to comfort him, she placed her hand on his arm.

Joao started, his gaze flicking to Saffie as sharp blades continued to lash at his insides. Confrontation with Pueblo had always been on the cards but he'd underestimated the older man's power to unsettle him even further. Or perhaps he was feeling it even more since he hadn't quite managed to return to an even keel since Saffie had announced she was leaving.

Or perhaps the answer lay in the features he'd looked into that had seemed so much like his own he'd spent an alarmed moment wondering what else he'd inherited from the man who'd sired him.

Was he deluding himself that he was the better man? Was his DNA programmed to repeat history and damn his relationship with his unborn children even before it'd begun?

He swallowed, a quiet terror rumbling within him he couldn't stop.

You're so much more than one man's opinion of you.

He wanted to cling to Saffie's words. But was he?

He'd shown that he could make money and wield his fortune with admirable expertise. But beyond that where else had he been tested? Certainly not on the emotional battlefield. He'd never let anyone close enough to test his mettle in that arena.

But you have a chance now.

Did he? His gaze fell to her slightly rounded belly, and the twin sons growing within her. He stifled the sharp yearning cloying through him. He still didn't know whether Saffie intended to take that chance from him.

But he could take steps to alter that. He could ensure he at least got a fighting chance.

He gritted his teeth, the determination to make that happen settling deeper into him.

Saffie watched as an expression shifted over his features, a betraying yearning, before he snuffed that out, too.

But that glimpse had rebirthed her wild hope.

Yesterday, he'd admitted he wanted her.

Could they not build on that? With a little time, couldn't she show him that, while their foundation had been based on the physical, there could be more? *They* could be more?

He turned to Lavinia. 'My apologies for the interruption,' he said.

The older woman shook her head, her gaze introspective. 'No need, Joao. There's a reason my own sons aren't by my side during this transition. Family is complicated.'

As if a switch had been flicked, the atmosphere lightened. Conversation flowed until Lavinia, having spent another fifteen minutes talking to Ernesto, suddenly turned to Joao. 'I understand there's another project of yours I need to see.'

Joao frowned, spoke sharply to Ernesto in Portuguese. The older man gave a sad little smile and responded. After another heated exchange, Ernesto shrugged.

Joao's lips firmed, displeasure clouding his face.

'What's going on?' Saffie asked.

'Ernesto insists on poking his nose where it doesn't belong.'

But Lavinia, sensing a rare weakening in her host, pressed her advantage. 'Forget another dinner party in my honour or whatever other wonders of your beautiful country you have in store for me. Show me this project and you will have my answer by morning.'

His lips firmed. 'This has nothing to do with our negotiations.'

'But it's everything to do with who you are,' Ernesto pressed with quiet, steely insistence that gave a glimpse of the willpower it'd taken to nurture an overwhelming personality like Joao's through the formative years of his life.

Joao didn't immediately respond and for the first time, Saffie spotted a sliver of vulnerability in the eyes that zeroed in on her and stayed. 'Joao? What are you talking about?' she probed.

His gaze shifted away, and she was left with the peculiar sensation that he was hiding himself from her, protecting himself from exposure.

'It seems I must rise to one final challenge,' he said tersely.

They left the stadium as they'd arrived, in Joao's helicopter. But with one further guest in the form of Ernesto, and a pregnant silence nobody seemed in the mood to break.

Flying north, they headed for the outskirts of Sao Paolo, where there were more wide open spaces than *favelas* and neat little houses that spoke to a middle-class neighbourhood. More untouched land spread beneath them for another few miles before the chopper started to descend.

The setting sun bathed the brand-new housing

development in golden colour as they landed in a large, beautifully landscaped park.

Saffie knew all of Joao's business concerns off the top of her head. This housing project wasn't one of them.

'Where are we?' she asked after he helped her out.

Ernesto smiled. 'Joao Cidade.'

Saffie's eyes widened. 'Joao City?' she translated.

'No one calls it that,' Joao interjected briskly.

'Except everyone who lives in it,' Ernesto parried.

She'd counted thirty blocks, set at architecturally pleasing angles from each other. About a quarter of a mile away, cranes and diggers were busy constructing another development.

The grounds were paved and landscaped, the apartments the kind that would command several hundreds of thousands in London.

Even before the chopper's rotors had quietened, a large group had formed in the park, families calling out to Joao in deferential greeting. He acknowledged the greetings with nods but he remained tense, his gaze darting repeatedly to Saffie's as they toured the nearest block.

They passed a small garden where someone

had carved *Joao Cidade* into a bench with hearts on either side.

Saffie stopped. 'Joao City…you built this, didn't you?' she whispered.

'He not only built and is still building five hundred homes per quarter, he gives them away free of charge to families from *favelas* all over Brazil every December,' Ernesto expanded with unmistakeable pride.

Saffie's jaw dropped. 'You do?'

'Extraordinary,' Lavinia agreed. 'Simply extraordinary.'

Joao said nothing, and when they entered an apartment large enough to comfortably house a mid-sized family, she watched him stride over to one window to look out onto a courtyard where a fountain splashed water onto cobbled stones.

'How long has this been going on?'

He tensed at Saffie's question and flicked her another neutral glance. 'I started the process eight years ago. Bureaucratic red tape meant it took another two years to get off the ground. The first phase finished eighteen months after that.'

'So you've been rehousing families for four years?' Mild shock coloured her voice. For a man who didn't want children and didn't believe in families, it was staggering. And the hope that kept wanting to push through surged again. Enough to draw shaky breath into her lungs.

Perhaps something of what she was experiencing showed on her face. He took a step towards her.

'Saffie—'

They were interrupted by a small commotion at the front door. Turning, she saw a pregnant mother with two toddlers clutching at her skirts hesitantly address Joao.

When he gave a curt nod, she entered, and Saffie saw that she clutched a bouquet of flowers. Tears spilled from her eyes as she spoke in rapid Portuguese.

Saffie didn't need a translator to know she was thanking Joao for changing her life. He withstood her effusive gratitude with a staid demeanour, only cracking a smile when one child came forward at her mother's urging to utter a solemn, *'Obrigado, Senhor Oliviera.'*

Saffie felt tears prick her own eyes. She quickly blinked them back, aware that Joao hadn't moved from the pillar of stone he'd turned into. For whatever reason, he'd wanted to keep this special deed under wraps.

Why, she didn't completely understand. But she could guess.

Deep down, Joao was attempting to rewrite

his own history. Giving back where he'd been cruelly denied.

She wanted to shake him, tell him it wasn't a weakness. One look at his stiff profile warned her against tackling it here. Now.

Ernesto and Lavinia rejoined them and they left.

They were halfway to the helicopter when she noticed he'd left the flowers behind.

Lavinia left within an hour of returning to Villa Sábia, but not before announcing her intention to sell her empire to Joao.

Joao's response was triumphant but curiously solemn.

The formal announcement was scheduled for Monday morning, Brazilian time. Saffie had already sent an approved press release to London and New York to be circulated concurrently.

Now, two hours later, she strolled onto the edge of the first-floor wraparound terrace of the north wing, her heart once again hammering with panic and wild hope. The sun had long set, cicadas wide awake and chirping in the gardens below.

Behind her, one of the two dozen bottles of Krug champagne she'd had placed in the wine cellar for this very celebration chilled in a silver ice bucket. The silk wrap she'd brought out in case the breeze turned cool trailed from her fingers as she strolled from one end of the terrace to the other.

This was more than a celebration for her.

This was the biggest undertaking of her life.

It wasn't every day you confessed your overwhelming feelings to your boss. To an extraordinary man like Joao—

'You've helped me win the biggest deal in my life, yet you pace like the world is on fire.'

She whirled, saw him lounging in the doorway, his eyes brooding, tension still vibrating off him. She wanted to ask why *he* wasn't celebrating.

But she wouldn't be veered off course, a feat he managed all too easily. To focus herself she dropped the wrap on a lounger and went to the ice bucket.

Small platters of Oscietra caviar on crackers, wagyu beef strips and grilled prime lobster bites were laid out on the table.

'I ordered these in case you were hungry.'

'How thoughtful of you.'

She slid a furtive glance at him. His smile as he sauntered forward didn't reach his eyes and she watched as he reached out to pluck the bottle from her nerveless hands with one hand while setting down a large, flat velvet box.

'What's that?'

'We'll get to that in a minute. You can't drink so what's the purpose of the champagne?'

'As you said, you've just closed a deal of a lifetime. I thought one of us should celebrate.'

His lips firmed, and he worked the cork until it popped. Weirdly, it was a flat sound that barely registered in the evening air. Saffie wondered if it was an omen. He poured out two glasses, set the bottle back and made no move to pick up his glass.

Instead, he reached for the velvet box. 'This is for you.' He held it out.

Saffie didn't take it. 'I sort of guessed it might be. I don't want it, Joao.'

His eyes narrowed. 'You don't know what it is.'

'It's another priceless trinket, offered with some sort of unnecessary ulterior motive for simply doing my job.'

Ignoring her, he pried the lid open. Despite herself, her gaze dropped. Along with her heart and her jaw.

Because, by far, this was the most stunning present he'd ever given her. The yellow diamonds were too many to count. He'd probably cleaned out Harry Winston's entire supply for this necklace, never mind the matching teardrop earrings, cuff bracelet and what looked suspiciously like an anklet.

'Why do you do this?' she whispered brokenly.

'I like to reward a job well done.'

'You don't need to buy me, Joao. I'm already—' She stopped herself at the last moment, self-preservation prompting her on a different path. 'Why did you keep the housing project a secret from me?'

The box snapped shut and he tossed it on the table as if it were worth nothing. 'Because it's no one's business but mine.'

The punch of hurt shouldn't have felt so disproportionately agonising, but it did. Because her feelings for him were larger than life.

'There's nothing extraordinary about providing decent homes for those who need them,' he continued with suppressed tension in his voice. 'It's a simple case of supply and demand.'

'Don't belittle your achievements, Joao, especially not one that clearly means so much to you,' she said softly. 'This is where you disappear to on Christmas Day, isn't it?'

Again he smiled an empty smile. 'Watch it. Next you'll be accusing me of playing Santa.'

'I wouldn't stoop so low. But I will say that while you may not think yourself a knight in shining armour, you're certainly theirs.'

'There you go, romanticising again. I'm not the man you take me for, Saffie.'

'There's nothing wrong with admitting that you wished someone else had done the same for your mother, that if you'd had somewhere to go maybe your childhood would've been less...'

'Less dire? Less horrific? What's the point of wishing? The past cannot be changed.'

'I know. But you're changing the present and the future. I just don't get why you feel it's something to hide.'

'There's a difference between keeping something private and hiding.'

'But why—?'

'Why would I not shout to the world that I'm the son of a prostitute? That my own father didn't want me?' he slanted at her, his voice a bleak desert.

'Joao—'

'Enough, Saffie. Do you still intend to leave me?' The question was raw, charged.

The urge to say *no* flew to her lips. She stopped herself at the last moment. 'That depends.'

A tic throbbed at his temple. 'I'm not good with ultimatums.'

She sucked in a sustaining breath, her palms growing clammy with the realisation that she had to navigate carefully. 'It's not an ultimatum. It's… I just want to know where I stand.'

His jaw rippled. 'You stand where you've always stood. At my right hand.'

Her heart dropped but she forced herself to go on. 'I don't mean with your work, Joao. I mean with this…thing between us. With our babies.' *With my heart.* 'I know you want to claim these babies as yours too but…' she licked dry lips, her heart hammering wildly '…will you do it with me in the picture, too?'

His eyes narrowed. 'What exactly are you asking me, Saffie?'

'You know what I'm asking. A proper commitment.'

He turned to stone. 'One bound in hearts and roses, perhaps?' he added bitingly. 'I'm sorry to disappoint you but that will never be on the table.'

'Why?' The question cried out from her fractured heart.

'Because I don't wish either of us to delude ourselves with frivolous emotions. Now I ask you again, are you going to stay?'

Her heart splintered into sharper pieces that made it harder to breathe. Harder to think. But he was waiting. And as much as she wanted to crumble, she had to stand her ground this one last time.

'No. The Archer deal is done. And so am I.'

He stared at her for several frozen moments. Then from his back pocket he produced a document. 'I had my lawyers draft an agreement.'

Her heart lurched. 'Why?'

'Because I have new interests to protect.' He set it down next to the jewellery box and turned away, abruptly. 'Read it. Then come to my study.'

He left the terrace without a backward glance, his untouched champagne turning as flat as her heart.

CHAPTER NINE

'IS THIS SUPPOSED to be a joke?' Saffie's voice shook like a leaf in a hurricane.

Joao didn't turn from where he stood gazing out of the window. Not for several pounding heartbeats when she walked closer, searching his towering frame for signs of humour.

There were none.

The gritty set of his jaw told her he'd heard her question. The intense gleam in the narrow-eyed gaze he'd finally directed at her when he'd deigned to face her told her everything she'd read in the agreement was exactly as he'd wished it.

'It's a legal document. What do you think?' he taunted, giving her all the confirmation she needed.

Her hand shook as she raised the document. 'It has to be,' she argued. 'Because it says that you're...' She stopped, swallowed disbelieving words she wanted to speak out loud. 'You're seeking custody of my babies!'

'They're my children, too, Saffie,' he corrected with icy patience.

'And…the date on this thing…it's the day after we found out…after the first ultrasound.'

'When have you known me to waste time on something I want?'

'So…your questions just now…you were testing me?'

His gaze clashed with hers, raw power blazing so fiercely, terror tap-danced down her spine. With deceptively casual steps, he approached, reached out and captured her chin, his grip gentle but firm. 'You're carrying my heirs, Saffie, and I'm claiming what's mine.'

The tap-dancing sped up. 'Stop saying that. They're not yours! If anything they're *ours*.'

He shook his head. 'Not if you plan on racing off into the sunset with them.'

She tried to speak but no words emerged. Not for several heart-pounding seconds. 'Please explain to me what's going on, Joao. Make me understand why, a few weeks ago, you ridiculed my intention to have these babies and now you're doing this!'

Again he said nothing for the longest time. Then his hand dropped. 'I told you, reality lends a different perspective.'

'I presented you with two shiny new toys and

now you can't help but take them away from me?' she demanded scathingly.

He stared at her for a moment before he sighed. 'I'd rather it not come to that.'

'But it will. Why?' That last word came out in a cringing, bewildered wail.

'I'm simply safeguarding my position. You will never have my agreement to take my children from me, Saffie.'

The document slid from her nerveless fingers, her whole body wracked in tremors. 'My God. To think I defended you to your father.'

'You shouldn't have. Perhaps I may be more his son than you bargained for. I see what I want and I go after it, consequences be damned. Doesn't that sound familiar to you?'

The question was harsh but she caught the barest glimpse of doubt in his eyes, as if he truly believed that about himself.

'We both know that's not true. And it's a little too late to hide behind his shadow. You've been your own man for a very long time, Joao.'

'Perhaps, but DNA speaks for itself,' he said. There was no remorse in his voice. Only true purpose.

'Is that what you intend to teach your sons? To accept that the apple doesn't fall far from the tree so they should accept whatever fate their grand-father and father's DNA hands them?'

His jaw clenched so tight, she thought it'd crack. 'They will never hear Pueblo's name from my lips.'

'That gives me my answer. I don't know if you're reacting to the meeting with your father—' She stopped, feverishly trying to read his face. Something bleak flitted across his face but again he wrestled it under control. 'You're letting him get in your head, Joao. But...even if I'm wrong, I won't sign this document. You know that, don't you?'

His face turned rigid. 'Then you'll be hearing from my lawyers.'

Bewilderment whipped through her. 'Why are you doing this? Was that what Shanghai was about? What these past few weeks have been about?'

His brows clamped together. *Do que voce esta falando?'*

'Don't give me that. You know exactly what I'm talking about. The sex...the public displays of affection. Were you softening me up for this... this hostile takeover?'

He strolled to his desk and sat, no, he *lounged*, owner and master of all he surveyed. But he didn't own her. Or her children.

Another tiny earthquake shook through her at the reminder that she was responsible for precious twin lives.

Lives he wanted to control.

'It won't be a takeover if we discuss it sensibly,' he said, confirming her fears.

'You want sensibly? Then tear up this document!'

He frowned. 'Calm yourself, Saffie.'

'Don't you dare use that tone with me. Not when you've been planning this for weeks. Take it back, Joao.'

'Will you stay?'

'No.'

A momentary flash in his eyes was all the answer she needed that he wouldn't shift from his stance. 'Then we have nothing else to discuss.'

She felt the colour drain from her face. But she took the tiniest satisfaction in ripping the agreement to shreds and tossing the pieces on his desk, even while she prayed the hot tears prickling her eyes wouldn't fall. 'Have a nice life, Joao!'

It was the party to end all parties.

Or so everyone insisted on gushing the moment he came within hearing distance.

His mansion tucked into the exclusive peninsular of Saint-Jean Cap-Ferrat was awash with dazzling lights, laughter and music that bounced off the still water. A quarter of a mile away, his superyacht was outlined by more dazzling lights, guests who wanted to see another area of his life partying on the decks of his vessel. Between the two venues, every imaginable whim was catered for by the expert hands of an executive assistant no longer in his employ.

Joao experienced a flash of acute, blazing irritation, which immediately snuffed itself out beneath the agony tightening his sternum and the heavy weight of his morose mood. But in its wake he felt searing loss the likes of which he'd never experienced before but had lately become a constant companion.

Three long weeks she'd been gone. But everywhere he looked, she lingered. Taunting him. Defying him with her absent perfection.

He stared down into the dregs of the cognac Saffie had convinced a French distiller to produce solely for him. Hell, he couldn't even drink now, or eat, or sleep in his own bed without being reminded of her every accomplishment. Her absolute perfection.

Behind him, world dignitaries and celebrities drank and danced on his dime as if there were no tomorrow.

While he suffered a thousand cuts of loss because the ache inside decimated him in ever-expanding agony.

He dragged a hand through his hair, absently noting its tremor, and the spine-cracking tension it took to hold himself together.

The greatest professional achievement of his life had arrived with a side serving of a pile of ashes in his mouth.

How he'd managed to conduct a sane conversation with Lavinia at the formal press conference yesterday, he would never know.

He'd made the right noises and confirmed he would safeguard her legacy.

And all the while, the colossal mistake he'd made regarding his own legacy mocked him mercilessly.

All the while, the woman who it turned out knew him more than he knew himself had taken herself out of his life with such ruthless efficiency, he almost admired it.

A remote private Caribbean island accessible only by invitation and not a single dime of her existence came via him. She'd rejected the Amalfi villa, returned all his jewellery and refused every single one of his calls.

His only glimpse of her so far was via a grainy picture of her on the beach, her hand cradling the sweet curve of her stomach where his children continued to blossom.

His children.

The ones his last encounter with his father had driven him to claim on a visceral but totally misguided level. His toxic encounter with Pueblo had fuelled a savage need for history not to repeat itself. Except he'd come at it from totally the wrong angle.

A deep shudder racked his frame, infusing every fibre of his being with the misery he hadn't been able to shake since Saffie's departure. Did he even have the right to call them his after what he'd done?

After brazenly believing he could fight this fate worse than death and plough on as if nothing had happened, only to compound his woes?

His staff cowered when he approached. The new assistant he'd hired irritated him with the simple, fatal flaw that he wasn't Saffie.

When midnight rolled around and the silence of whichever office he happened to be in oppressed him, none of his residences felt remotely like home.

Not without Saffie.

His fists balled, the anguish that even thinking of her name brought ravaging his insides.

She'd opened her heart to him, laid bare her

most precious wish. A wish that ran parallel to one he'd been unwilling to admit to.

To be better versions of the lives imprinted on them.

Instead he'd taken it and soiled it.

Now it was too late.

He heard footsteps approach but didn't turn around. 'Monsieur Oliviera? Your guests are waiting for you on the terrace so the fireworks can begin.'

His fist tightened so hard he felt a bite of pain. But this pain would never come close to the one in his heart. And he couldn't live with it. Not any more. 'Tell them I have better things to do. They can all entertain themselves.'

'Monsieur?'

'Call my pilot. Tell him to get my plane ready.'

It might be too late but he needed to hear her say it to his face.

The richest man in the world had, with the Archer acquisition, solidified his position once and for all, leaving his nearest competition in the dust.

Saffie set aside the newspaper screaming Joao's success, his sheer brilliance and a dozen more superlatives. She shouldn't have opened the paper. Shouldn't have given into the temptation for just one more glimpse of him.

Even thousands of miles away, the man could so very easily devastate her.

She struggled to calm the agonised roaring within, then realised the rush of sound wasn't in her head.

It was coming from outside, and growing louder by the second.

Standing, she went to the French doors to the villa she'd rented for the month, the beauty of the space not registering.

It would've been easier to return to her Chiswick flat, attempt to make the space she'd never truly lived in a loving home for when her children were born.

Except it'd been far too close to where she'd given four years of her life to Joao. She wasn't ready yet to share a metropolis with him. She might not be for a long time.

The sound grew louder. Deafening. Opening the doors, she stepped out. 'What's going on?'

One of the caretakers turned to her. 'There's a helicopter approaching.'

She frowned at the looming speck. Watched it whip up the sand on the beach and then simply...hover. 'What's it doing?'

'Attempting to land, miss.'

Her heart dipped for reasons she couldn't explain. 'But...there's no helipad. Doesn't he know how dangerous it is?'

The caretaker glanced from her to the aircraft and back again. 'I don't think he particularly cares, miss.'

She frowned. Then her heart began to hammer. Only one person would attempt the kind of magnificent recklessness the pilot was exhibiting. Only one person would brazenly come here uninvited like this.

She was sorely tempted to instruct her housekeeper to call the authorities. But if she knew nothing else, she knew Joao wouldn't give up. His silence in the past weeks had merely been the lull before the storm.

And the storm had arrived.

Her hand slid protectively over her stomach, the quiet astonishment and awe at how rapidly her babies were growing filling her heart before searing anguish emptied it.

'Miss? Shall we call the police?'

She refocused on the chopper, watched it slowly pivot until the pilot was in clear view.

Hovering fifty feet off the ground, Joao stared at her from behind the controls.

Swallowing thickly, she shook her head. 'No. Let him land.'

As if he'd heard her, the aircraft descended immediately, sending the tops of the palm trees swaying wildly as the blades whipped the air and the chopper settled on the lawn.

Unable to stay and watch him, let him see how desperately she'd missed him, how the sight of him both thrilled and frightened her, she turned and fled indoors.

Joao found her in the living room, the sight of her close up, the curve of her stomach beautifully visible, glowing with health even while her eyes flashed hurt and fury at him, stopping his breath for an age.

'*Você é linda*, Saffie,' he whispered reverently before he could stop himself.

'Brava on your spectacular entrance. But know that I've instructed the housekeeper to alert the authorities if you're not off this island in the next thirty minutes, so don't waste your time telling me I look beautiful.'

He raked a hand through his hair. 'I will risk jail if you would hear me out.'

He watched her debate for an eternity before waving him to the seat farthest from her.

'Saffie…the things I said…the things I did in Sao Paolo…'

'Deplorable things I will probably never forgive you for.'

He held tightly to the *probably*.

'I was a boy who came from nothing and had nothing for more than half my life. I didn't want children because deep down I didn't think I would be in any way a fit enough father. And frankly, the thought of giving something so vital of myself terrified me. But…when we found out in Shanghai that you were pregnant, things changed. I wanted them, but admittedly not for altruistic reasons, initially. Even then, Pueblo fuelled my reasoning. Because what better triumph than to show the old man everything he'd done wrong with the bastard son he'd sired, then callously rejected, than to be the better father than he could possibly be and rub his face in yet another failure? Succeed where both he and my mother had both failed so abysmally?'

Understanding flitted across her face. But there was also pain. Disappointment.

He swallowed. He held out his hands, pleading without words for her understanding. 'I've never made a deal when I walked away with nothing. You threatening to walk away, first from being my right hand, and then with my child—'

'Our children.'

'*Sim.* Two of the most precious things I've ever

helped create… I just reacted the only way I knew how. Then coming face to face with Pueblo after so many years in Brazil…'

She frowned. 'When was the last time you saw him before the match?'

'The first time I bested him in a deal I was twenty-four. I insisted on him being there to sign the company I'd just bought from under him. Sao Paolo was the next time. After almost a decade, I'd fooled myself into thinking I'd be able to handle it. But you were right. I let him get to me. And believe me, I heard what you attempted to tell me that night in Sao Paolo. You were exposing every part of myself I've striven to hide and, well… I'm learning to accept some of it. Because to trust so completely…was another new phenomenon I couldn't contemplate.'

'But you trust me. At least in part.'

'I trust you wholly. It was simply easier to delude myself that the professional front was the only one that mattered. Confessing after that I wanted to do things differently, learn to love where I wasn't loved, was far too exposing. The agreement was the perfect way to attempt to leave my emotions out of it.'

'But you couldn't.'

He gave a low, self-deprecating laugh. 'Did

I not manipulate you to ensure I would have a hand in your life even if you left me?'

Her stunning eyes swept away from his, her hands cupping her shoulders in self-protection that made him feel like the lowest of the low. 'I hear all of this. But how do I trust you now? After everything that's happened?'

Pain slashed his insides as he slowly approached her. 'By giving me a chance to prove myself. I stood the lawyers down the day you left. The precious children you carry will bear whatever name you wish them to bear. All I ask is that you give me a role in their lives. That you give me a chance to be their father by not owning them, but by loving and cherishing them the way every child deserves. But…if you don't want me to have anything to do with them—'

Her fingers on his lips stopped his words. 'I would never do that. Not after what we've both been through. That was what I'd planned on telling you that night on the terrace. That I wanted us to co-parent our babies. That even if you didn't have…feelings towards me you would at least love *them*. I needed that commitment from you for them, Joao. Because anything less than that won't do.'

A deep shudder shook him to his toes and he

squeezed his eyes shut. 'The most valuable deal of my life and I messed it up spectacularly.'

Soft hands found his jaw and he pried his eyes open. 'It's not too late. If you meant what you just said. If you're willing—'

He caught her hand in his, infusing his vows through touch. And then through words. '*Meu Deus*, yes. I'm willing, Saffie. More than.'

Her eyes dimmed. 'So this is just a co-parenting role you want?'

'What right do I have to ask for more?'

'Has that ever stopped you?'

'*Meu amor*, I may not be bright when it comes to…certain things but I'm a quick learner. I will stop if—'

'You're brazen. You're cunningly clever and you're scarily ruthless when you need to be. Don't let me down now, Joao,' she urged huskily.

He heard the plea in her voice and his heart began to hammer against his ribs. 'Saffie…are you…?' He swallowed, for the first time in his life unable to voice his need.

'Ask me, Joao,' she insisted.

He sucked in a breath, and laid it all on the line. 'I want to be more than the father to our children. I want your heart. I want your trust. I want the right to call you mine and to love you as you deserve to be loved. With adoration. Completely. For as long as I draw breath.'

He held his breath as she stared back at him. As her eyes filled with tears. As a sob broke free and she threw herself into his arms.

As he caught her and held her and experienced the first, true taste of homecoming.

'So, how was the party?'

Joao nuzzled his face deeper into the sweet curve of her throat, the need he'd thought sated after four hours in bed with Saffie astonishingly rising again.

'I don't know. I left half an hour after it started.'

She gasped, moved back to look into his face. 'You didn't.'

Now, well into her second trimester, she glowed with the health and beauty attributed to a lucky few pregnant women. But he liked to think there was an extra-special something that made the woman of his heart a vision in his eyes.

'Without you it wasn't a celebration. And I don't care about anyone else there as much as I care about you. Only you. I love you, Saffie.'

Tears she'd blushingly attributed to hormones filled her eyes again. 'I love you, Joao,' she sighed against his lips. They kissed for an eternity before he raised his head.

'Besides, I have a feeling I've been a little… scary lately. People flinch when I approach. I need you to come back and…soften my edges.'

She laughed. And it was the best sound in the universe. A sound he wanted to roll in. Replicate until it played in an endless loop in his soul.

'You've proved conclusively that you have what it takes to remain the richest man in the world. People are bound to be intimidated whether I'm around or not.'

'I don't care about being the richest man in the world. I care about being the best husband to you.' His hand glided over her stomach and his breath strangled all over again. 'The best father to these two and however many we have in the future.' He looked up, deep into her eyes. 'Marry me, Saffie. Make me the happiest man in the world?'

Again her tears spilled. But she nodded through it, her husky, *'Sim. Para sempre sim,'* making his own eyes prickle.

They made love again, and just as she was about to drift off he reached for her hand and performed one last task.

Saffie's eyes opened, then widened as she saw the large, exquisite diamond ring on her finger. 'Now this piece of jewellery I love. Just as I love you.'

Her eyes met his and she gave him a smile that woke his soul and promised him eternity.

EPILOGUE

Four years later

'JOAO? WHAT ARE YOU—?'

Saffie's steps slowed as her husband raised a finger to his lips in a *hush* gesture. She paused, studying his expression.

Half amused, completely besotted, he flicked his attention away from her after a second. She smiled, knowing what was absorbing his attention as she tiptoed down the hall in bare feet towards where he was leaning on the wall next to the door that led into their twin sons' bedroom.

His gaze flicked back to her, lingered on her full breasts, her hips, down to where her peach-coloured night slip ended mid-thigh. When he raised his gaze again, his eyes were filled with the fierce carnal heat that hadn't dissipated an iota since that first time they'd made love on his divan in Morocco.

It was their first night back in their estate on the outskirts of Sao Paolo. It was good to be back home but she was exhausted and had been waiting for her husband to join her in bed. His continued absence had sent her in search of him.

A noise drew his attention back to their sons' room. Joao held out his arm and silently motioned for her to join him.

Smiling, Saffie tiptoed past the doorway, and melted into her husband's side. After he'd dropped a quick kiss on her lips, they peeped together into the room where identical twins, Carlos and Antonio, stood face to face.

'Watch,' Joao murmured.

They were engaged in a heated argument, three-year-old Carlos holding aloft his favourite toy, a blue whale he never travelled without. In his hand, Antonio held his second favourite toy. As he blabbered in toddler Portuguese, Antonio started to reach for the whale. A frantic argument broke out.

Saffie started to disengage but Joao held her back. 'No, *meu querida*. Watch,' he insisted under his breath.

The two boys babbled for another few minutes. Then Carlos haltingly held out his blue whale. After a few seconds, Antonio walked off and returned with his red toy truck. They exchanged toys, then the grinning boys fell into each other's arms, laughing in triumph.

'A month ago, they would've fought like wild horses. They're learning negotiation skills,' Joao said, pride stamped in his voice and on his face as he drew Saffie fully into his arms.

She wound her arms around his neck. 'I don't think they're quite ready for the boardroom yet, Joao.'

He brushed his lips over hers, eliciting a thrilling shiver that drew a smug smile to his lips. 'Perhaps not, but they're learning to fight for what they want and not walk away until they're satisfied.'

'A bit like what you did with their *mama*?'

He slanted his mouth over hers and kissed her for a long, wickedly thrilling minute before raising his head. *'Exatamente.'*

With a suave move that left her breathless, he swung her into his arms, paused to check that the nanny was overseeing their sons, before carrying her down the hall to their bedroom.

He laid her out on the bed, then shrugged out of his polo shirt and cargo pants in two smooth moves. Naked, he prowled over to join her. Elbows braced on either side of her head, his eyes burning bright, he stared down at her. 'Tell me you're satisfied, *meu coração*. Tell me I've made you happy?'

It still stunned her that a man as powerful and

charismatic as Joao sought reassurance from her. That her happiness meant so much to him. But somehow it did.

'Words cannot truly express the joy you bring me, Joao. But perhaps I can find a few for what I need to tell you.'

His eyes feverishly probed hers. 'What is it?'

She caught up one hand, brought it to her lips and kissed his scarred palm. Intertwining their fingers, she drew them down to rest on her stomach.

His breath audibly caught. 'Saffie?'

Tears prickling her eyes, she leaned up and kissed him. 'I went to see Dr Demarco today. I'm ten weeks along.'

Whisky-gold eyes caressed her face, then dropped to her stomach. '*Meu Deus*. I thought I knew what happiness was. You've just shown me a whole new dimension.'

They shared a slow, languorous kiss, during which Joao managed to divest her of her negligee. She welcomed him home, waited until he was deeply seated inside her and they were frantically catching their breaths before she delivered the final news.

'There wasn't just one heartbeat, Joao. There were two. We're having another set of twins.'

His whole body visibly shook and Saffie caught

a glint of tears in his eyes as his mouth dropped reverently over hers. 'Saffie. My Saffie. With you my cup has truly run over. *Eu te amo muito.*'

'I love you, too.'

* * * * *

LET'S TALK
Romance

For exclusive extracts, competitions
and special offers, find us online:

- **f** facebook.com/millsandboon
- 📷 @millsandboonuk
- 🐦 @millsandboon

Or get in touch on 0844 844 1351*

For all the latest titles coming soon,
visit millsandboon.co.uk/nextmonth

Want even more
ROMANCE?

Join our bookclub today!

'Mills & Boon books, the perfect way to escape for an hour or so.'

Miss W. Dyer

'Excellent service, promptly delivered and very good subscription choices.'

Miss A. Pearson

'You get fantastic special offers and the chance to get books before they hit the shops'

Mrs V. Hall